A Bent Creek Redemption

Harker Brothers Ranch Book 2

Catie Cahill

Contents

Come Home to Bent Creek   VI

1. Chapter One   1

2. Chapter Two   5

3. Chapter Three   10

4. Chapter Four   17

5. Chapter Five   23

6. Chapter Six   27

7. Chapter Seven   33

8. Chapter Eight   39

9. Chapter Nine   45

10. Chapter Ten   50

11. Chapter Eleven   56

12. Chapter Twelve   61

13. Chapter Thirteen   65

14. Chapter Fourteen   70

15. Chapter Fifteen   75

16. Chapter Sixteen   80

17. Chapter Seventeen   86

18. Chapter Eighteen   90

19. Chapter Nineteen   96

20. Chapter Twenty   99

21. Chapter Twenty-one   101

22. Chapter Twenty-two   108

23. Chapter Twenty-three   111

24. Chapter Twenty-four   119

25. Chapter Twenty-five   125

26. Chapter Twenty-six   130

27. Chapter Twenty-seven   136

28. Chapter Twenty-eight   143

29. Chapter Twenty-nine   148

30. Chapter Thirty   153

31. Chapter Thirty-one   158

32. Chapter Thirty-two   161

33. Chapter Thirty-three   166

34. Chapter Thirty-four   169

35. Chapter Thirty-five   172

36. Chapter Thirty-six   175

37. Chapter Thirty-Seven   181

38. Chapter Thirty-eight 185

39. Chapter Thirty-nine 189

Epilogue 193

More by Catie Cahill 198

About Catie 199

Come Home to Bent Creek

A SMALL TOWN IN Montana where everyone knows everyone, secrets live in the shadows of the mountains, and love is just waiting to be found. One by one, the Harker brothers return home to reclaim their ranch, face their family's past troubles with the Nobles, and find the love they didn't know they needed.

Chapter One

Emily

My roommate was missing.

Okay, not *missing* missing, as in I should've notified the police or anything. She stopped coming home almost a week ago in favor of staying with her boyfriend. Except she hadn't bothered to check in with me at all since then.

Mom told me she'd seen Anna at the Snowshoe Café on Saturday, and Larkin at the coffee shop mentioned Anna had been in to get her usual cold brew on Monday morning. But that was three days ago now.

"Leo, do you think I should call the police about Anna?" I looked up from my computer behind the library's main circulation desk to where one of our two volunteers, Leo Thomas, was reshelving books in the New Titles section.

"Anna?" He wrinkled his brow, and I bit my lip to keep from laughing. Leo was maybe forty—hardly old enough to be so forgetful with how many times I talked about my roommate. But his head was usually up in the mountains somewhere with the off-the-grid cabin he was building.

"My roommate," I reminded him. "The one who hasn't been home in a week."

"Are you worried about her?"

"No . . . Maybe. She's with her boyfriend, I think. And other people have seen her. But it's weird that I haven't heard from her in so long. It's like she's ghosted me." I looked at my phone again, as if a text from Anna would magically appear.

"Did you go to her boyfriend's place?" Leo asked.

"No." That was an obvious solution, but I didn't really like Anna's boyfriend. Steven wasn't mean to her, but just . . . lazy. Always asking her for money and coming over to eat our food. How he managed to keep his own apartment, I didn't know.

Leo nodded, satisfied he'd given me some kind of solution to my problem, and wheeled the cart around to the next aisle.

I glanced down at my phone again and opened the string of text messages I'd sent Anna over the past few days. She hadn't replied to any of them, and that's what was so weird. I typed out another one, hoping that maybe she'd lost her phone and hadn't gotten a new one yet.

If I didn't hear back, I guess I was going over to Steven's later on.

I sighed at that thought and set my phone down before standing up to stretch. The Bent Creek Public Library was only open for another half hour, and all of the usual patrons had already cleared out. It was slow enough that I thought I'd go ahead and do my closing rounds.

I smiled at the literary quotes hanging on the walls and the bright colors in the children's section. I loved this library more than just about anything. Coming here with my sister when we were little, it was like an oasis away from the hustle of Main Street outside. In here, it was warm in winter and cool in summer, and I could lose myself in any story I wanted. When kids were mean at school, I jumped into a story about a girl who could save the day. When I lost my dog, I read stories about brave animals and the kids who loved them. When I was a teenager and couldn't seem to get a guy to notice me, I'd read book after book about boys falling for the quiet, nice girl.

This library was my home away from home, and the fact that *I* was now in charge of it seemed like a dream come true.

A dream that didn't pay much, but that was okay. That was why I lived with a roommate and didn't go crazy shopping online or eating out. Some things were more important than money.

Although I wouldn't exactly say no if some handsome, rich knight sauntered in and swept me off my feet.

I laughed quietly at that as I reorganized the baby board books in their brightly colored cube shelves. It was hard to imagine something like that happening in Bent Creek, where I knew everyone. My knight would have to be a tourist, because it wasn't like the guys I already knew were breaking down the door to ask me out.

You're too quiet, Emily, my sister Sabrina would say. *How would anyone ever know you're interested if you don't actually talk to them?*

I bristled at her voice in my head as I picked up a stray sippy cup from the squishy chairs in the corner. I *talked* to people just fine. I just didn't do it a lot because, well . . . I didn't know what to say. But it wasn't like I was afraid to talk to them.

Okay, unless it was a guy and he was really hot. Then I got kind of tongue-tied.

I dropped the sippy cup into the lost and found box behind the circulation desk and picked up my phone. Ten minutes to close—and I'd missed a call from my landlord.

I frowned at my phone. Why was he calling me? Anna's name was the one on the lease, so she got all the rent reminders and messages about repairs. I was about to hit the call back button when the library door opened.

And the last person I ever expected to walk into the Bent Creek Public Library strolled inside my doors.

He paused, pulled off a pair of sunglasses, and looked around until his piercing gaze landed on me.

"You hiring?" Jackson Harker asked.

Chapter Two

Jackson

Emily Foley blinked at me like I'd asked the question in Russian.

I folded my sunglasses and stuck them in the pocket of my jacket before moving closer to the desk. Jerking my thumb over my shoulder toward the door, I added, "Saw the sign on the door."

Her honey-brown eyes flicked toward the door, then back to me, and suddenly I feel like I'd never left junior year homeroom. I'd recognized her the second I walked in. I never had classes with Emily—she was smart, I was bored—but she sat next to me in homeroom the last year I went to school in Bent Creek. Never said a word to me, but I never forgot those eyes.

"Oh, that . . ." Her voice trailed off, and I could almost hear her thinking. "It's . . ."

She didn't look at me as she tried to come up with an excuse. I took another step toward the desk. The library wasn't my first choice in employment, but I needed money, and it was the only place in town that had an opening where I didn't already have some kind of history. Mostly because I hadn't stepped foot inside these doors since I was a little kid.

She finally looked at me again, and I noticed she had a sprinkling of freckles across her nose that matched the color of her eyes.

"We filled that position," she finally said as she rested her phone on the desk.

I narrowed my eyes just slightly as I watched her. She glanced away from me and swallowed visibly.

I took one more step, dropped my hands onto the desk, and leaned forward. "You're lying."

Her attention shot back to me. She tilted her head, her mouth open slightly. I'd surprised her, and that made me smile, even if the reason for the lying burned like it had happened yesterday instead of years ago.

"I . . ." She trailed off and then wrenched her mouth shut as her cheeks went pink.

I didn't move. Something about making Emily Foley uncomfortable was giving me a strange sort of joy. Besides, she looked awfully cute when she got flustered.

"I'm not lying," she finally said. "We have Leo." She gestured to a cart parked at the end of an aisle of books.

"I'm a volunteer," a muffled voice announced from behind the shelves.

I smirked at the announcement before turning back to Emily. Her frown deepened.

"Yes." She pressed her palms against the edge of the counter before fixing her gaze back on me. "All right, fine. What are you reading right now?"

"I just got here. I don't have any reading material yet." Or much of anything else to my name.

"Okay, what's the last book you read?"

"Mmm . . ." I leaned against the counter. "What's that one with the two people who are in love but they can't be so then they kill themselves?"

She blinked at me. "Are you talking about *Romeo and Juliet*?"

I slapped my hand on the counter. "That's it. That was depressing, wasn't it?"

"We read that freshman year of high school."

"Yeah. Heck of a thing to throw at a bunch of fourteen-year-olds. All that murder and suicide."

She bristled. "It's a *classic*."

"Not saying it was bad. Just depressing." I shrugged.

Emily shook her head like she wasn't enjoying this conversation nearly as much as I was. "I asked you about the last book you read, Jackson."

"I answered it. And hey, you remembered my name." I gave her a grin.

"Of course—" She shook her head, cutting herself off. "Are you seriously telling me the last book you read was thirteen years ago?"

I shrugged again. "Is that a bad thing?"

Her eyes widened and she lifted her hands, gesturing at the space around us. "You're applying for a job in a library. Where there are *books*."

Her irritation made me smile. "I know what a library is."

She dropped her hands and blew out a breath between her teeth. The air made the hair around her face lift, and it took everything I had not to laugh. I wasn't getting this job, but I was sure enjoying myself in the process.

"Okay, so . . . I have to tell you that you're not really qualified to work here," she said, all professionally.

"Really?" I pulled a pained expression.

"Yes . . ." She frowned slightly as she realized I was putting her on. She sighed again and pulled the hem of the yellow and white striped top she was wearing. It was cute—all sunshine and summer and with a V-neck I could definitely appreciate.

"Look," she said, drawing my attention back to her face. "I think the hardware store is hiring. Why don't you try there?"

I couldn't keep the wry twist from my lips. "Old Man Lewis still run that place?"

"Yes."

"Yeah. That won't work." Another spot to avoid. I pocketed more than one item from Town Square Hardware as a teenager. Melvin Lewis confronted me about it once, but I denied it and he had no proof. There was no way I was walking back in there, even if I'd long outgrown petty theft.

I tapped my hand on the counter. "I'll see you around, Emily."

"Are you staying very long?" she asked.

I paused and turned back around, the grin finding its way to my face again. "Why? You want me to?"

"No," she blurted out, her face going a deeper shade of pink this time. "I mean . . . My roommate's boyfriend got a job with the construction company working on the Summit Mountain Ski Resort expansion. You could try that."

I studied her a moment, enjoying the way she kept moving her hands from the counter to her phone to her hips. Nerdy Emily Foley had turned into someone *very* interesting.

"Thanks," I finally said. "I'll see you tomorrow."

I could feel the look on her face as I left without glancing back. And somehow, I felt a lot better about coming back to this town than I did before I saw her.

Chapter Three

Emily

Jackson Harker was *the* most irritating man I'd ever met.

And he was taking up way too much space in my head as I picked my way over puddles in the parking lot. Spring was finally here, and the last of the snowbanks that had piled up all winter were melting furiously.

Why? You want me to? I rolled my eyes at the memory of his words. The worst part was, I couldn't tell if he was flirting with me or if he just liked making people feel uncomfortable.

And that was just ridiculous. Did it matter? There was *no* way he was actually flirting with me—he never even glanced my way in high school. Even if he was, did I really want attention from someone like him?

I shoved away the thought of how his lips curved up in a teasing smile every time he'd looked at me. I had bigger issues going on—like, where was my roommate?

Jogging up the stairs to our second-floor apartment, my keys jingling at my side, I hoped she was finally back. If she wasn't . . . I cringed at the thought of knocking on Steven's door. But at least I could reassure myself she was okay, even if she was ignoring my texts.

I reached our door and lifted my key to the lock, barely registering how shiny the doorknob was. Maybe the landlord had finally done something to improve the place.

The landlord! I'd completely forgotten to call Keith back after Jackson Harker had left.

I jiggled my key in the lock. Nothing happened. I pulled it out and tried again, but the lock wouldn't turn. Frowning at the door, I reached for my phone. Maybe this was what Keith had wanted to tell me, that the new lock was sticky or that I needed to pick up a new key.

I found his number and leaned back against the wall as the sound of ringing echoed through my phone. A breeze wafted over the rusted iron railing, carrying the scent of spring, damp and full of promise. I closed my eyes, reveling in the moment, until Keith Tarrant picked up the phone.

"Tarrant," he said.

I straightened up, jarred back into reality. "Hey Keith, it's Emily Foley in number ten. On Lodgepole Street. I—"

"Yeah, Emily. Hey." He sounded like he had ninety other things he'd rather do than talk to me. There was a rustling at the other end of the line and then, "Your stuff is in a storage unit. I can meet you there whenever."

"My . . . what?"

"Your stuff, from the apartment. Tell your mom I'm not a complete asshole." He chuckled as I squinted at the doorknob. My mom had babysat half the town years ago, but whatever she thought of Keith wasn't exactly what I was worried about at the moment.

I lifted my key again and tried the lock. It wouldn't budge. My heart fell like a piece of lead into my stomach.

"Emily?" Keith's voice echoed through my phone, sounding a million miles away even though he was probably somewhere just across town. "You okay? You've got another place lined up, right?"

My breathing turned shallow. "So this means . . ." I couldn't finish the sentence.

Keith didn't answer me right away. "The eviction went through, yes," he finally said, very carefully, as if he was afraid this was news to me.

Because it *was* news to me.

I grabbed my keychain so tightly that it dug into my palm. The pain kept me from having a full-on panic attack at my sudden lack of a home.

"Yes, okay." I breathed the words into the phone. "Thanks. I have to go now."

I hung up before Keith could say anything else. Did I really just thank him for evicting me? And how did we get evicted in the first place?

I shoved my phone into my pocket and pressed my hands against my burning cheeks. I felt so stupid. How did this happen without me knowing anything? I paid my half of the rent every month to Anna. What did she do with the money?

And how did I not *know*? There had to have been notices on the door. And Keith would've called . . . I squeezed my eyes shut. He would've called Anna. Her name was on the lease, not mine. He called me today as a courtesy, just to let me know about my stuff.

My clothes, food, toothbrush, everything I owned was in that storage unit now. I had *nothing*.

Anger bubbled up in my chest. I needed answers. *Now.*

Steven's apartment was just a few minutes away, like everything in Bent Creek. I parked on the street in front of the duplex he rented and stormed up the driveway. Anna's car was parked next to Steven's at the top of the driveway.

"Anna!" I shouted her name as I pounded on the door.

No one answered.

I knocked again, louder this time.

Breathing hard, I glared at the bright red door, which remained firmly shut. A red door was a sign of welcome, I vaguely remembered Mom saying. But I felt anything but welcome now.

Anna was ghosting me. She took my money, got us evicted, and now she didn't even have the guts to come to the door.

I stepped backward away from the tiny porch, not sure what to do next.

"Emily?"

I whirled around. Larkin Reyes stood on the sidewalk, her little son's hand clutched in hers.

"Hey," I said weakly, trying to force a smile as I moved toward my car.

Larkin tilted her head. "Are you okay?"

I probably looked like a wreck. Smoothing down my hair, I made my smile bigger. "Yeah, I'm good."

She held my gaze a moment as Diego bent down to examine a crack in the sidewalk. "Are you sure?"

I didn't know Larkin well, not enough to unload all my problems on her, but the way she looked at me made it seem like she'd be the kind of friend who'd be your rock when your world fell apart around you.

I wished I had a friend like that.

I swallowed, and slowly shook my head. "It's not a big deal. Just . . . well, I got evicted from my apartment and my roommate . . ." I trailed off, not wanting to dump out everything on my mind. I barely knew

Larkin beyond getting a coffee at Mountain Roasters once in a while or seeing Diego at the library's story time. We weren't even in the same class in high school.

Her eyes widened in understanding. "Do you need a place to stay for the night? I'm right down the street."

It was the nicest offer anyone had ever made me. My heart ached at the kindness. "No," I said, even though my brain was screaming *yes*. "I'll just go to my parents' house. But thank you."

She smiled at me as Diego's attention left the sidewalk and he tugged at her hand. "Of course."

"Mama, Nick!" Diego pointed a chubby finger down the sidewalk. Larkin's attention turned in that direction, and her smile brightened.

I glanced down the road and spotted a man in a cowboy hat leaning against a truck in a driveway several houses down the road. Larkin was dating Nick Harker again, I knew from gossip. People didn't have a whole lot to talk about in Bent Creek, but they sure did like talking about the Harkers.

My mind immediately went back to Jackson Harker, taking up all the space in front of my circulation desk. How had I not heard about him coming back to town?

Unless he'd just arrived.

My heart thumped weirdly at the thought of being one of the first people who'd seen him in town.

"Let me know if you need anything," Larkin said, interrupting my thoughts.

"Thanks," I replied, and she waved before letting Diego drag her down the sidewalk.

My eyes flicked toward Nick, who seemed to be waiting for them. And that made me think of Jackson again.

Quit. I shook my head as I opened the door to my car. I needed to stop thinking about him. It wasn't like he'd sought me out in particular or anything. He was looking for a job, that was all. I'd gotten through high school barely thinking about him, so I didn't know why I couldn't do the same now.

All that self-assured hotness notwithstanding.

I started the car and gripped the steering wheel. I didn't have time to think about cocky, good-looking men who were the epitome of bad news right now. I had to figure out more important things, like why Anna didn't tell me about the eviction. And where in the world I was going to stay tonight.

I drove mindlessly down the road, passing Larkin and Nick as they embraced next to his truck. I didn't know where I was going.

To Mom and Dad's. *No.* Of course they'd let me crash in their guest room. But not until after a long lecture from Dad about my career choice and how it stacked up next to Sabrina's. Breakfast would come with a healthy serving of *I told you so* and *You're so smart. Why didn't you go to law school?* and *By your age, your mom and I were married with a house and a baby on the way.* Mom would look on sympathetically, never judging me herself. She was more than supportive of how much I loved my work at the library. It was Dad I couldn't face.

I mentally ticked through everyone I knew as I made my way back toward Main Street. Sabrina lived in Denver—and even if she was here, staying with her would be like staying with a female version of Dad. My best friend Callie had moved to Houston with her boyfriend two years ago, and I wasn't even sure I could call her my best friend anymore. Pretty much everyone else I was close with had left town while I was gone at grad school. There was Leo, but we didn't exactly hang out after work or anything, so asking him would be seriously weird.

I bit my lip as I sat at a stop sign. There were a few hotels down by the interstate. I had enough cash for three or four nights, at least. But they'd ask for a credit card, and the one card I had was almost maxed out. Just the thought of standing there while it got declined made my face go hot. I could just picture a hotel clerk running into Dad and saying, "Oh, I saw Emily yesterday! She tried to get a room but her card declined. Is everything okay?"

A horn sounded from behind me. I lifted my hand to wave a "sorry" and spotted the mayor waiting behind me.

Sometimes Bent Creek was just the right size—and sometimes it was way too small.

I drove aimlessly for a few more minutes before pulling into the municipal parking lot on Main Street, where I sat and tried to figure out what to do.

The library? We had a little break room with an ancient couch. And a security system owned by the town that I'd have to turn off, which would probably go into a log somewhere, and then I'd find myself explaining to the mayor or a police officer about why I was at the library in the middle of the night.

I thumped my head against the steering wheel. Where was I going to go?

I could drive back and take Larkin up on her offer, which sounded more awkward than I was willing to deal with.

Or I could sleep in my car.

Chapter Four

Jackson

"Here goes nothing." Nick grabbed hold of the doorknob and pushed his weight against the door.

"Nothing's about right," I said when the door didn't budge.

Nick took a step back, looking up at the place we used to call home. "For a house that looks like it's ready to give up, it's putting up a hell of a fight."

"It knows where it came from." I gave my brother a half smile.

He shook his head, but he knew what I meant. You didn't grow up as a Harker in this town without walking away harder than steel.

"We could break a window," Nick said, rubbing a hand over his face. "But then we'd have to fix it, and there's plenty enough to fix already. And it would turn this into a legit crime, according to Gabe anyway."

"One of them's probably unlocked." I turned the doorknob again, rattling it hard. It gave a little this time. I pulled out a debit card to a mostly empty bank account and fitted it into the crack between the door and the frame.

"Put that away." Nick's voice was sharp.

"It just needs a little help." But he was right. *A little help* would cross the fine line between legal and not.

Nick eyed me for a moment, that big brother crease in his forehead growing deeper by the millisecond, as I stood and slid the card back into my pocket. "I don't want to know why you knew how to do that."

"You don't," I agreed. I gave the knob another strong twist, this time lifting up as I turned.

And it gave. With a groan worthy of a ninety-year-old man, the door swung open.

I held out my hand, gesturing for Nick to go inside first. "Look at that. It was unlocked. Not technically breaking and entering. But maybe trespassing," I added in a cheerful voice, like adding crimes to my list was what kept me going.

Nick pointed a finger at me as he finally stepped inside. "Not that either."

"Whatever you need to tell yourself to sleep at night." Gabe had sworn up and down that this was all perfectly legal, but it sure didn't feel that way. I pushed aside a dangling cobweb from the doorway as I followed Nick inside.

Nick didn't say anything, and once I shook the web from my hand and looked up, I knew why.

Memories wheeled through my mind, so fast I had to suck in air to push away the stinging in the corners of my eyes. The wall where my stepmother Katrina kept an end table with a long, draping tablecloth. I used to hide under it from Nick and Gabe when I was little. The spot by the door where Pops would kick off his boots at the end of the day. The staircase with the loose newel.

Seeing it again was somehow comforting, and yet felt like someone had taken a knife and twisted it hard in my intestines.

"At least it's empty," Nick said in a hollow voice. "No furniture or anything."

"Yeah." If the place had looked enshrined in time, it would have gutted me.

"What a mess." He took a few steps farther inside.

I followed his gaze up to the ceiling, where it looked like a pipe must have burst ages ago from the bathroom upstairs.

He led the way through the living room to the kitchen. I gripped the doorframe and gritted my teeth against the onslaught of memories. Clear as day, I could see Katrina stirring a pot on the stove while Colt and Mav begged her for a cookie or a snack pack pudding. I saw myself sneaking out the back door to meet whatever girl I was seeing at the time, or tossing on a coat from the rack that still hung by the door to go help Pops in the barn or in the warehouse he'd put up in the far wooded part of the property.

Pops. I hadn't talked to him in years. I'd thought about it. Even thought of driving to that prison in California, but I didn't. What would I have said when I got there?

I swallowed the feelings that came with all the memories as Nick strode across the room, running a hand over the decrepit-looking stove.

"Wonder why they took the fridge and left the oven," I finally said. It was a weak attempt at humor.

Nick shrugged. "Looks like you've got company." He jerked his chin toward the corner by the door.

Mouse droppings. Great. "I don't suppose you're offering an exterminator with that air mattress and bag of groceries?"

"Adopt a cat."

"Maybe I will." Although when I tried to picture myself sitting in the living room with a cat and no one else around, it felt so off that I shut it down. "Or maybe I'll hire an exterminator with my big bucks construction job."

"You could've worked cattle with me and Gabe," Nick said as he made his way back to the living room.

"No way in hell." I never minded working around the ranch, but I drew the line at working with the cattle. They had it in for me. Maybe that's why it was so easy for me to slip into Pops' other line of work.

Or maybe I was just meant for trouble.

Nick laughed. "Let's get my truck unloaded."

I followed him out the front door, noting how he'd avoided going upstairs. I couldn't say as I blamed him. Just seeing the first floor was almost more than I could handle.

And somehow I managed to let Nick and Gabe talk me into staying here.

"You knock over a grocery store?" I asked as I peered into the bed of Nick's truck.

"You can blame Larkin. She didn't want you going hungry."

I knew I always liked that girl.

"Here, I grabbed this too." Nick pulled a portable charger from one of the bags once we got back inside. "You'll have to charge it in your car, but it should help keep your phone going."

Right, because I was about to live without electricity. And indoor plumbing. It was like camping, but with more trespassing.

"This one's also got a camp stove, some lanterns and flashlights, batteries. Pistol, just in case."

"Just in case," I repeated as I set my bags down. Just in case of what, I didn't want to think about. But this was Bent Creek, and our history here was long and messy. "Thanks."

I moved to the window, assessing the distance to the road. The big pine out front blocked some of the view, and as long as I kept the window covered, no one should see me from the road at night. "You sure no one comes by here?"

"Positive. Gabe and I staked it out a few nights to make sure. That Chestnut Moon company just lets it sit abandoned."

"Five years," I said, more to myself than to Nick. It was plenty of time to get the place into shape.

"Five years and it's ours, according to Montana law. So long as no one notices us paying the taxes on the place."

I nodded, still looking out the window at the fading light. The scheme Nick and Gabe cooked up was squatting. Live in a place, fix it up, and pay the taxes. And if no one kicks you out, you can claim the property after five years.

It wasn't like I had anything better to do. Or anywhere else to live. So squatting in my own family's old house was it. Could have been worse.

"I have to meet Larkin for dinner. You need anything, let me know." Nick paused by the door. He smiled. "It's good to have you home, Jackson."

Something in me broke. I'd *missed* him. Him and Gabe and the others, but mostly Nick. We were two of a kind for so long, until everything fell apart. He'd always had my back. I felt like I barely knew him now, but also like nothing had ever changed between us.

"Jail," I said before I could change my mind. "Back when you called, you asked where I'd been. That's where I was."

Nick nodded, not a sliver of judgment in his expression. "I'll stop by tomorrow," he said.

After he left, I ran a hand through my hair, surveying the bags on the floor. I had an air mattress to blow up, and Larkin had included a canvas bag full of blankets. I had to get the food put up somewhere away from the mice.

But instead of doing any of that, I wandered back to the stairs and looked up. Halfway up the stairs, a book lay abandoned. I moved up the stairs just far enough to pick it up. Blowing the dust off the cover, I read the title.

The Tempest. By William Shakespeare.

I laughed, loud and lonely in the empty house. Who knew where this came from. If it was left over from one of us, or left behind by some teenage vandal who'd broken in years ago. There was one other place it might've come from, and I glanced up at the dark landing, wondering if it was possible. It couldn't be. The place was empty aside from this book.

Freaking Shakespeare, though. It made me think of Emily Foley, and the appalled look on her face when I told her I hadn't read any-thing since high school. It was a lie. I wasn't a big reader, but I'd read a book here and there over the years. But it was more fun to see her reaction when I told her I hadn't.

I wonder what she'd say if I told her I was back for good.

I laughed again, this time at myself as I tossed the book back onto the step and headed downstairs. I wasn't ready to go all the way up. Not yet.

And I definitely had no business thinking anything more about Emily Foley.

Chapter Five

Marybeth

LARKIN RAISED A CUP of coffee in greeting.

"You're my favorite person," I said when she reached my storefront and handed me the cup. It was warm against my hands, and I relished the feeling of it against my skin as the morning chill hung in the air around us.

"Of course I am," she said with a grin. "Just don't tell Gabe. Did you get everything unpacked yet?"

I made a face as I took a sip of the sweetened coffee. "Mostly, but I didn't realize how much stuff we didn't have." I'd gotten rid of most of the things I had before when I'd moved back in with my brother. And Gabe gave away most of his stuff instead of hauling everything here from Chicago. Now that we'd moved in together, we were missing so much. "Like a blender. I had no idea we didn't have a blender until I'd already chopped up a bunch of fruit to make a smoothie yesterday."

"We might have an old one I can give you," Larkin said. She glanced down the street, past Bent Creek Christmas, toward the town square. But her eyes didn't focus on anything in particular.

"How are things between you and Nick?" I asked carefully. "Is he still . . .?"

"Talking about marriage? Yup." Larkin sighed and brought her eyes back to me. "I just wish he'd slow down, you know? It's not that I *don't* want to . . . just not yet."

I nodded at Mayor Barry as she hurried past us. She taught my brothers in high school before being elected, and before that, I remembered her working the dunking booth at the county fair to raise money for kids with special needs. She also made sure I stayed in business by ordering the town's Christmas decorations from my shop.

I turned back to Larkin, my mind returning to her and Nick. "Have you told him that?"

"I've hinted at it, but he's *so* excited."

"Larkin." I gave her a look.

"I *know*. Okay, I'll be more direct." She glanced behind her, back toward Mountain Roasters where it looked as if rain was threatening to fall soon. "I've got to get to work."

I waved at her and leaned against the doorframe of my shop. Bent Creek Christmas had survived winter by a thread. Now I had to figure out how I'd get through the slower summer season. I sighed and straightened. Maybe the answer would come to me while I worked today.

"Hey, Marybeth." Emily Foley, the town librarian, paused in front of my shop, a plastic drugstore bag in her hand. The wind picked up and tossed her light brown hair every which way.

"Hey! How's the library?" I asked, keeping the fact I had a very overdue book back at my new house to myself. Moving was chaotic, and I'd just dug it out of a box a few days ago.

"Oh, it's good." She looked distracted, her eyes flicking down Main Street and back again. "Hey, do you need anything for your new place? Like . . . furniture or kitchen stuff or anything?"

I hid a smile. This was how it seemed Bent Creek worked. A problem came up, and there, out of the blue, was someone to help with it. And of course she'd know I'd moved in with Gabe. Nothing stayed a secret very long here. "Yeah, actually. Gabe and I keep finding little things we need." I furrowed my brow as her meaning sunk in. "Are you moving away? I don't know what the library would do without you."

"Oh! No. I mean, I'm not leaving town. I just . . . Yeah, I'm moving. Just, here. To somewhere else."

She seemed weirdly nervous, but Emily had always been on the quieter side. I don't think I'd ever talked this long with her before. Maybe she just got anxious talking to people.

"Okay, well . . . Can I make you a list or something?"

"Yeah, that would be great. I really need to downsize." She smiled gratefully at me. "Just, um . . . Can you text it to me?"

I nodded, and we exchanged phone numbers. I waved at her as she hurried down the street, the wind pushing her along. She looked relieved, and I couldn't tell if she was just glad to find a home for some of her stuff, or if something else was going on with her. I wished I knew her better so I could ask.

A crack of thunder sounded from above, and I ducked inside the shop just as the first raindrops began to fall. I leaned my forehead against the window in the door, watching the rain splatter on the sidewalk and the road as I thought about the day ahead.

Organize inventory. Swap out one of my trees for a spring-themed tree. Hopefully wait on customers, if the rain didn't drive them away. Run by the grocery. Stop by the ranch to grab the boxes of old stuff in the garage I'd left behind.

That wasn't something I looked forward to at all. Things between my brother Luke and I had been strained ever since I told him I was moving in with Gabe. Not that they weren't strained before, when Gabe and I had first started dating. And then even more when I found out he'd been keeping a huge, awful secret from me my whole life. This was just the latest fraying in the rope that tied us together as siblings, and I was afraid the entire thing would snap if he didn't ease up and just let me live my life.

Maybe I could get in and out of the garage without running into Luke at all. Because despite what I'd told Larkin earlier, sometimes avoidance was the easiest option.

Chapter Six

Jackson

Nails. A hammer. Screws. A Phillips head and a flat head.

That was all I needed, but it might as well have been gold chains and diamonds. I stood across the street from Town Square Hardware, Nick and Gabe's cash sitting useless in my pocket. There was no way I was going in that store. I was too old to get the stink-eye from Mr. Lewis.

"Mornin', ladies." I nodded at the two older women I vaguely recognized from my childhood as they walked by, obviously staring.

If my greeting took them by surprise, they didn't show it.

"Good morning, Jackson," one of them said, undisguised curiosity leaking from the edges of her voice.

I nodded again. Bent Creek, where no one forgot your name, even after eleven years, and even though you had brothers who looked like you. It was unsettling and reassuring at the same time. But mostly unsettling, since I could guess exactly what they thought of me and my brothers.

Yanking my phone from my pocket, I checked the time. I only had a couple of hours before I needed to be at work. I had to get this stuff now, or I'd be listening to that hanging piece of siding all night and cursing the sticky doorknob on the front door every time I went in or out.

I needed someone to buy it for me.

I considered my options as I looked up and down the street. Nick and Gabe were working. Larkin was too, although at least she was in town. I could ask her to go on her break, but then I'd have to come back into town to pick everything up after work. My eye caught Bent Creek Christmas a few storefronts away, and I frowned. I trusted my brother Gabe, but I wasn't convinced about Marybeth yet. She was still a Noble, even if she was living with Gabe.

That left . . . no one.

My gaze caught a slender figure not too far down the sidewalk, ponytail swinging and a bag falling off her shoulder. And I smiled.

Maybe there was someone else.

"Hey, Shakespeare." I fell into step next to Emily as she walked toward the library.

She startled, clearly not expecting anyone. "Hey. Wait, what did you just call me?"

I grinned at her. She wore a black jacket over a V-neck that looked a lot like the one she had on yesterday. I wouldn't ever forget that shirt. "Shakespeare. I have a favor to ask you."

She paused. "Shakespeare was a poet. A playwright. I'm a librarian."

"It's all books," I said with a shrug.

"It's all . . ." she repeated before shaking her head. "You mentioned a favor? I still can't hire you."

I let out a short laugh. "I'm good there. Got hired on at the resort. Thanks for that tip, by the way."

She flushed slightly, which made my brain go in six different directions it shouldn't. "Could you buy something for me?" I pulled the money from my pocket to show her I wasn't asking her to pay.

"Like what?" Her eyes flicked to the wad of cash in my hand.

"Some stuff at the hardware store. Nails. Hammer. Nothing too crazy."

"Okay . . ." She sounded as confused as she should be. "So why can't you buy it?"

"Trust me, I just can't. Shouldn't take more than five minutes. Do you mind?"

Emily glanced down the road at the library. "I have to open in a half hour."

"Plenty of time," I said with my most winning smile.

The corners of her lips turned up just slightly. I guess I hadn't lost that charm yet. "All right, fine. Just nails and a hammer?"

I gave her the money and rattled off the list. Her eyes scrunched up as she tried to remember it. It was unexpectedly cute, and I had to shove my hand into my pocket to keep from reaching up and using my thumb to smooth out the lines at the corner of her eye.

As she moved across the street to the hardware store, I shook my head and tried to figure out what it was that intrigued me so much about Emily Foley. I still didn't have an answer when she emerged a few minutes later, bags in hand.

"Change," she said, dumping bills and coins into my hand. "And the stuff you wanted. Do you need it for work?"

"No." I shoved the change into my pocket. "For the place where I'm staying."

She raised her eyebrows, clearly curious. Can't say I wasn't feeling smug about the fact she wanted to know more about where I was living.

"It's kind of a dump," I confessed.

"Ah," she said. "Well, that explains . . ." She waved at the bags in my hand.

"Yeah."

She looked up at me then, a spark of something in her eyes. Worry, sadness, fear—I couldn't gauge it. But those eyes . . . I didn't know what to call them. They were this bright golden brown. The only reason she didn't stop every guy in his tracks in high school was because she was so darn quiet, always looking down or away from people. But now . . . With that soft hair and that sweet smile, the way she put me in my place in the library—there was no way she didn't have a boyfriend.

"Amber," she said out of nowhere.

"What? Is that your middle name?"

"My eyes." She shifted, casting her gaze down just as she'd done all through school. "That's the color. People are always curious."

Warmth crept up the back of my neck at the way she read me so easily. I didn't think I was being obvious, but here I was, doing the same thing every other person did when they met her.

"That's not the only thing they should be curious about," I said, trying to backpedal from being just one of the masses. And why I was trying so hard, I didn't know.

Who was I kidding? I knew exactly why I wanted her to see me as different. *Shut it down, Harker.*

But I didn't. Instead, I raised the corner of my mouth into a half smile that usually made women slink a bit closer.

Not Emily, though. She swallowed, so my ladykilling grin wasn't entirely lost on her, but she didn't cave. Which somehow made me want her more, despite every warning bell going off in my head.

"Christine," she said, lifting her chin.

I blinked at her, stumped for the second time in just a few minutes.

"My middle name. You wanted to know, right?"

It wasn't the only thing I wanted to know. I was falling dangerously close to something I would have a hard time pulling myself back out of. "Emily Christine." I tested the words on my tongue and nodded.

"So." She crossed her arms, clearly waiting for something from me. "What?"

"Usually when you tell someone something like that, they give you the same information about themselves."

"I see." I paused, letting the second stretch. "My eyes are brown."

She looked at me a moment and then made this laugh-snort. She covered her mouth as her cheeks went pink, and it took everything I had not to laugh myself.

"I didn't know you were so funny," she said as the flush faded from her face.

It was so genuine that I didn't know what to say. No woman had ever called me funny. Intense, moody, and even annoying as hell, but never funny. Was it something they'd never noticed, or was it that Emily brought it out of me?

Whatever it was, I liked it.

"You never really knew me at all," I said finally.

She pushed her lips together, thinking. "No, I guess I didn't. I didn't know a lot of people."

The bells at the church down the street began to ring, but I couldn't take my eyes off of Emily. I'd looked right past her in high school. And I'd been a fool.

"I have to go," she said.

I nodded and held up the bags. "Thanks for this."

"You're welcome." She turned to go, but then stopped. "I'm going to want the answer, you know."

"The answer . . . To why I asked you to buy this stuff for me?" I held up the bags, weighing whether that truth would make her curious or send her running back to her library.

"Oh . . . yeah. I do. But I was talking about your middle name."

My middle name. A grin stretched across my face. "That's a secret you'll have to pry out of me. But there are ways . . ."

Her eyes widened slightly and she shook her head in exasperation before striding away. But halfway down the block, she glanced back. I nodded at her, and she spun back around, not stopping.

I shifted the bags to my left hand and turned back toward my car, unable to wipe the smile from my face.

Because I had a suspicion Emily Foley wanted me as much as I wanted her.

Chapter Seven

Emily

I DIDN'T WANT THE day to end.

My neck ached from sleeping in my car last night, and as the minutes crept along toward closing time, I still didn't have an answer to what I'd do for tonight.

I slapped the barcode on a new book and sighed. At least I knew my stuff was safe. I'd asked Keith earlier if I could have a few weeks to get everything straightened out, and he was okay with that. Apparently he kept the storage unit for furniture and appliances. My stuff—and I guess Anna's, unless she snuck over and got it all out while I was at work yesterday—wasn't taking up that much space. Maybe I could at least give some of it to Marybeth to make it less of a burden for Keith to hang on to. He even said he wouldn't charge me for it, although I was pretty sure that was because he felt guilty for evicting me since he knew my parents.

My parents.

I added the book to the stack next to my computer and picked up the next one. I couldn't sleep another night in my car, and Mom and

Dad's house was the obvious place to go tonight. But every time I pictured it in my head, all I could see was Dad's profound disappointment. And an hour-long lecture full of *I told you so* and comparisons to my sister. Followed by regular doses of *the Look*.

I just couldn't do it. I'd sleep a week in my car before putting myself through that.

At least barely being able to sleep last night, in between moving my car to different locations to avoid unwanted knocks on my window, had given me time to think through my situation. I needed a roommate. That was the only way I'd be able to get another apartment on my meager library salary.

I wonder if Jackson needs a roommate.

My face flamed at the thought. Where had that come from? I didn't know, but I didn't dare think it again.

"Are you okay? You're quiet today. More quiet than usual, I mean." Leo paused by the circulation desk. He waved at Mr. Yardley, the older man who was leaving after his daily stop to use the library's internet.

"Fine," I said quickly, forcing down the lingering embarrassment over that random thought about Jackson. "Just tired."

Leo nodded and thankfully asked no more questions. He headed away with a stack of books toward the cozy reading area in the middle of the library. I sat back in my chair and pressed my hands to my face. Jackson Harker was trouble on two legs, and that was the last thing I needed right now.

Ha. As if I'd ever even be in the position to turn him down. He was a flirt, and that was it. His type was less librarian in an Old Navy ensemble and more street racer in tight jeans and tattoos. I liked to go no more than five over the speed limit and hated the thought of needles. I was decidedly *not* the kind of girl Jackson would ever be interested in. He probably just didn't know how to talk to a woman without flirting.

And *why* was I thinking so much about him when I needed to figure out my disaster of a living situation?

It was the car again tonight unless I came up with another solution. If I could find a place like the library but without the alarm system, that could work. Somewhere no one would come looking in the middle of the night. Some place that people left alone. Somewhere . . .

An idea formed in my mind. Maybe there *was* a reason I couldn't stop thinking about Jackson Harker. One that didn't have anything to do with those dark-as-sin eyes and that chiseled jaw.

I sent Leo home early and took my time closing up. Thankfully, I'd shoved a bunch of microwaveable meals into the break room fridge two weeks ago before everything fell apart. I heated one up for my dinner. Then I brushed my teeth with the toothbrush I'd bought that morning and took a makeshift bath at the sink.

What I wouldn't give for a real shower. I never knew the things I took for granted until I didn't have them anymore. A bathtub. Cabinets filled with food. A closet full of clothes.

I wrapped the toothbrush in a paper towel before putting it, the toothpaste, a hairbrush, and a stick of deodorant back into my purse. I had to get some more clothes. Leo probably hadn't even noticed I was wearing yesterday's clothes again today, but I felt sticky and uncomfortable. There was a thrift shop up by the interstate. I could probably make my pathetic amount of money stretch there until I could arrange to meet Keith and get some of my clothes.

That was where I'd stop first. Grab a few things to wear, then go to Walmart for a flashlight, a blanket, and a pillow. Maybe a big bottle of water too. That shouldn't cost too much. And then I'd see about the crazy plan I'd hatched earlier while sitting behind my computer.

Fifty-two dollars and ninety-eight cents later, I was the proud owner of the barest of necessities. I sat in the Walmart parking lot while the sun went down, shivering with the sudden drop in temperature. I charged my phone while I tried to convince myself that my plan wasn't really that outrageous.

I had to do it. It was that or face Dad, and I'd rather sleep on the ground and freeze than deal with his opinions.

Drawing in a deep breath, I started the car and pointed it back toward Bent Creek. The shadows of evergreens gave way here and there to moonlight as I turned onto Quarter Mile Road. The closer I got, the harder my heart thumped. I couldn't remember exactly how far down the road it was. I eased up on the gas, and the staccato rhythm of the moon and dark trees slowed with me.

Finally I found the right turn. Gravel crunched under the tires as I pulled into the empty driveway. My car sputtered when I silenced the ignition, and I winced. I didn't need car trouble along with everything else.

The sudden silence filled my ears as my heart pounded. The old house was straight ahead, with empty, blank windows and dark gables that reached toward the velvet sky.

I shuddered, and then rolled my eyes. Who was I turning into, Edgar Allen Poe? I laughed at myself. There were no eternal beating hearts or talking ravens lurking in the old Harker house. It was just wood and drywall and shingles. That was it.

It was just a place to stay for a few days while I found a new roommate. And I was grateful it was still standing and the windows weren't busted out.

Pressing my lips into a determined line, I scooped up my purse and my shopping bags before pressing the car door open. The usual spring night sounds were oddly silent, which only lent to the creep factor surrounding this house. My teeth chattered, and I wished I had my coat instead of this lightweight jacket that I hadn't bothered to actually zip up. It felt like winter was settling back in. An owl hooted somewhere in the distance, and the breeze rustled the evergreen branches overhead.

I can do this.

One foot in front of the other, I made my way to the porch and the creaking steps, eager to get out of the cold even if the house was haunted. I just wished it wasn't *so* dark. Maybe if I got my phone light on, I'd feel better.

Shifting my bags to my left hand, I fumbled for the phone I'd shoved into my pocket. Light on, I held it awkwardly as I reached for the doorknob. My fingers wrapped around it, but I didn't turn it.

What if it was locked?

And why didn't I think of that until now?

This was a bad idea. Creepy old house in the middle of nowhere. And it probably *was* locked. I should've just swallowed my pride and reached out to Larkin. Or sucked it up and gone home to my parents.

Something about that last thought made me tighten my grip on the doorknob. If it was locked, I'd try around back. And if that was locked, I'd try the windows. I wanted so badly to stretch out and sleep tonight.

And with the thought of sleep, I turned the knob.

The door opened immediately.

That was easy. I took a step forward, nudging the door open farther with my toe. What if it was *too* easy? What if the fact that it was open meant people snuck in here to . . . to . . . I didn't know, wait on women to come by, all alone and vulnerable? A hundred awful possibilities sprouted in my head.

I stood in the doorway, blinking into the darkness before remembering I had my phone light. I dropped the bags just inside the door and held up the light to look around.

There was a mess of blankets in the otherwise empty front room. I swallowed. So people did sneak in here. *Probably just teenagers*, I told myself, pointedly ignoring the images of wild-haired, toothless, ax-wielding murderers tumbling through my mind.

I tightened my grip on the phone and forced myself to move forward, toward the rear of the house. I should've brought a knife or some mace or *something*. Just in case. I could just see the headline now. *Evicted librarian tries to fight off wild-haired, toothless ax-wielding murderer with old cell phone and practical purse.* A smaller typeset beneath that said, *If only she'd listened to her dad and gone to law school.*

I gritted my teeth as I stepped across the threshold into what looked like a kitchen. I scanned the light around. Coat rack. Back door. Cabinets. Countertop with cans and boxes. Stack of paper plates. Oven. Missing space that should have held a fridge.

Wait. I swung the light back toward the countertop. A box of Froot Loops stood open next to a bag of potato chips, some hamburger buns, several cans of Coke, and a six-pack. And there was a bag from the hardware store. I blinked at it. Teenagers wouldn't leave—

"Turn around slowly and tell me what the hell you're doing in my house."

Chapter Eight

Jackson

THE PERSON HESITATED JUST a fraction of a second before doing the exact opposite of what I said. He—she?—spun around so fast I couldn't even see their face before the light from their phone blinded me.

Instinctively, I threw up my left hand to block my eyes while my hand tightened around the Glock that Nick had brought.

The person screamed, and the light went out as something clattered to the floor.

"Please don't shoot me!" a woman's voice squeaked out.

Blinking into the sudden darkness, I let the pistol drop a little as my vision slowly returned. The woman stood in the middle of the kitchen, hands up, and . . . she looked familiar. The sliver of light from her phone on the floor combined with the moonlight through the windows illuminated long brown hair and a V-neck shirt under an open black jacket. I blinked again and dropped the gun to my side. "Emily?"

Her eyes were wide and her mouth opened once, twice, before she finally spoke. "I'm sorry. I didn't think anyone . . . I didn't know you would . . . The door was open, and—I'll go. I'm sorry."

She moved faster than I expected. But as she tried to brush past me to leave the kitchen, I stopped her with a hand to her shoulder. "Wait."

Her eyes, darker in the shadows, flicked from my hand on her shoulder to the one holding the Glock. I set the pistol down on the counter next to me and lifted my hand to show her it was empty.

"What are you doing here?" I asked as her eyes found my face again.

She hesitated, and I could almost see her trying to decide whether she was going to tell me the truth.

"You can let go of me now," she finally said, her voice a little breathy.

I dropped my hand, silently cursing myself. "Sorry I scared you."

"I wasn't scared," she said immediately.

I lifted an eyebrow at that. "You almost ran out of here without your phone."

Emily's gaze immediately went to where she'd left her phone, face down, on the floor. "Oh." She scooped it up while I waited, arms crossed, in the doorway to the living room.

She turned off the flashlight and shoved it into her back pocket before striding back toward me. "Um . . . Can I get through?" she asked when I didn't move.

"Not until you answer my question."

She sighed as if she was annoyed at me, but she wasn't doing a good job of covering up how she really felt. There was something else. I leaned a shoulder against the doorframe, assessing her.

"What question?" she asked, even though I knew she was stalling.

"You didn't forget."

"Then what are *you* doing here?" she countered.

"It's my house."

"I thought they took it after . . . you know . . ." She trailed off, and I realized what it was she tried to hide so badly.

She was nervous.

My heart cracked, and those old feelings of self-loathing slid in. *I* made her nervous, and it wasn't because she was attracted to me.

"After my father went to prison?" I finished her sentence.

She hesitated a second, then nodded as she fiddled with the strap of her purse.

"Yeah." I dropped my arms, hoping it made me look less menacing. "Look, you don't have to be afraid of me."

"I'm not afraid of you," she shot back immediately.

"You look like the slightest noise is going to send you running to cower in the corner."

She narrowed her eyes at me. "I wouldn't *cower*."

My mouth twitched, and I had to work to keep from grinning at her indignance. "So when it comes to fight or flight, you fight?"

"I—" She shook her head. "Never mind. I need to go."

"Not until you answer my question."

"Answer it yourself. Why are *you* here? And where's your car?" She crossed her arms and lifted her chin. And I decided that quiet Emily Foley would definitely fight, which was a surprising—and intriguing—thing to learn about her.

"I'm parked around back." To keep anyone from knowing I was here and kicking me out. "And it's my house," I said again.

"Except it's not."

"How do you know? Have you looked at the deed lately?" The deed, which clearly stated I was *not* in any way the owner of this property. I was bluffing and hoping she'd buy it.

Emily glared at me for a moment, arms tightly crossed over her chest. Then she dropped her hands and shrugged. "Fine. I don't have anywhere else to go, and I thought this place was empty. Clearly, it's not. So I'll go and leave you alone."

She made for the door again, and this time, I turned to let her through. Her shoulder brushed my chest for the half second we were both in the narrow doorway, but I barely registered the moment because I was too focused on what she'd said.

"Are you serious?" I asked. "You don't have anywhere to stay?"

She sighed, her shoulders drooping as she scooped some plastic bags up from the floor. "I was evicted. I shouldn't have said anything. Forget it. I'll be fine."

She looked anything but fine. She looked exhausted.

I wondered what she'd do if I stood in front of her and opened up my arms. Would she fall into them and press her cheek to my chest, or would she shove me as hard as she could and go running for the door?

No distractions, I reminded myself. Not with the massive project that was this house—and my wreck of a life. But I pressed on anyway. "Sorry, can't forget it now that you said it. What about your parents?"

"No." She shook her head and looked off to the side, avoiding my gaze. "I'm not . . . I'll go back to my car. It's fine. Sorry I bothered you."

I swallowed the question on my lips. I was the last person who needed to interrogate anyone about their messed-up family situation. Although I was dying to know how a girl from a family beloved by the town, a girl who grew up here and stayed, the good girl town librarian, had no one to lean on.

No distractions, my brain echoed as my mouth said, "Stay here."

Emily's eyes widened. "No. This is your place. I can't . . ."

I stepped forward until I was right in front of her, just as I'd pictured earlier. But instead of opening my arms, I leaned forward as if I was going to tell her a secret. Her breath caught, but she didn't move. I counted that as victory.

"This isn't my house. Not yet. Which means you have just as much right to stay here as I do."

I leaned back to see her reaction.

She blinked at me as if she were seeing me for the first time. Then she shook her head. "This was a bad idea. It's illegal. I shouldn't have—I *really* have to go." Her voice ratcheted up a notch on each word, until it was nothing but a squeak.

Before I could say anything in response, she spun around and made for the door. Throwing it open awkwardly with the bags in her hands, she stepped outside as a blast of cold air rushed in.

An involuntary shiver rattled me from head to toe. I'd been outside working all day, first at the resort, and then on the door here in the little time I had before the sun set. It had been mild, good for outdoor work. Nothing at all like the Arctic air that blasted in from the front door now.

The door remained open, and I finally spurred myself into moving forward to close it—only to find Emily standing stock still on the front porch.

Was she having second thoughts? My heart leapt annoyingly, and then I saw what had stopped her.

Snow.

And not just a few flurries. It was coming down hard and fast. The moonlight lit up the driveway, which was already covered. It wouldn't be long before the yard was too.

Emily redoubled her hold on her bags and started toward the porch steps.

Was she seriously getting in that car? It looked like it would slide off the road if it hit an ice cube.

"Wait!" I said.

She paused and turned back toward me, the icy wind lifting the ends of her hair.

"You can't go out in this." I gestured at the snow.

Emily gave me a look that clearly said I was crazy. "It's Montana," she said slowly. "I can drive in the snow."

"Which means you should know better than to go out in a car like that when the snow is coming down this fast."

"It's not that far to town." She started to turn again.

"Yeah, and you'll freeze before the night's over. Or are you going to your mom and dad's?"

That made her stop. I could practically see the warring emotions on her face. Finally, she pressed her lips together and turned back toward me.

"Fine," she said. "But just for tonight."

As I held the door open for her, it seemed as if I'd won some kind of battle. The problem was, I didn't know what war I was fighting.

Chapter Nine

Emily

This was the single most awkward thing I'd ever done in my life.

It felt like I'd walked into one of the romance novels lining the paperback carousels in the library. One of those books where the heroine drives her car into a snowbank during a blizzard and has to be rescued by the gruff yet sexy mountain man. They find themselves stuck in a cabin in the woods together while the storm rages outside, and of course there's only one bed and—

"Mayo? Or are you a ketchup person?" Jackson interrupted my increasingly embarrassing thoughts by holding out a container of mayonnaise.

"Oh, um, mayo. Thanks."

"Good, because I don't have ketchup." He gave me that dangerous half smile, and my brain went right back to romance novel material.

My stomach rumbled as he assembled the burgers he'd grilled on a propane camp stove. I'd missed the cooler in the corner when I'd come into the kitchen earlier. It was chock full of ice and food. Somehow, Jackson made this whole living without electricity thing work.

He dumped a few potato chips onto a paper plate and handed it to me. Then he gathered up the battery-powered lantern, his plate, and shoved a couple of Cokes under his arm before leading the way out of the kitchen and into the living room.

"Fireplace seat?" He gestured at a patch of empty floor by the cold fireplace.

"Don't mind if I do," I said, and I found myself smiling despite the absurdity of all of this. I made myself comfortable and took a bite of the burger. My eyes closed, and I groaned at the heavenly taste. "This is incredible."

"You're easy to please," he said, swallowing his own bite.

"I'm starving," I admitted. That little frozen meal I'd eaten at the library was enough to stay alive, but that was about it. "And this is *really* good. What did you put in it?"

"Secret recipe," he said with a wink.

We ate the rest in silence. My stomach happily full, I set my plate down on the floor and stretched out my legs while I leaned back on my hands.

"So, you're starving and you got kicked out of your apartment." Jackson reiterated the facts of my sad life while he stretched out his own legs. His work boots sat awfully close to my worn Nikes. I clenched my muscles to keep from accidentally letting my foot fall sideways against his.

"Basically, yes. But it won't be for long." I just had to find a roommate. And go apartment hunting for something affordable. And hope Keith had kept my name off the eviction proceedings with the court system since the lease was in Anna's name.

"And you don't want to go home."

"No." I cast a sharp look in his direction. If he was going to be nosy, so could I. "So are you going to tell me why you're here, since you confessed to not owning this place?"

He lifted a corner of his mouth. "You really want to know?"

"Yeah, unless you're running a trap house or something," I joked.

And I realized a second too late that I'd said the wrong thing. Jackson's devilish half-grin faded into a frown, and even in the LED glow of the lantern, I could see a flicker of pain dance across his face before disappearing into something practiced and hard. He glanced away.

"I'm sorry. I shouldn't have . . . I was joking and I forgot about the rumors . . . " I stumbled over my apology, probably making it even worse.

"It's fine," he said, sharp and final. "That was a long time ago."

I nodded as a giant gust of wind rattled the windows. Cold snaked in through every crack and crevice, and I felt it more now that I wasn't thinking so much about how hungry I was. I pulled in my legs, crossed my arms over my chest, and rubbed my hands over the backs of my arms.

Jackson stood, crossed the room, and came back holding something in his hand. "Here." He stood over me holding out a fleece-lined coat.

"Thank you." I was too cold to even think of saying no. So instead, I stood and put the coat on over my jacket, sinking gratefully into it. It was long enough to cover my hands and the tops of my thighs, and I withdrew into its folds like a turtle into a shell.

"It's late," he said, glancing at his phone. "We should get some sleep."

I nodded, my face peeking out over the collar of the coat. He still hadn't told me why he was here, but it felt like that moment had passed.

"Ladies first?" He held out his hand toward the mess of blankets I'd seen when I had first walked in. I hadn't noticed then that there was also an air mattress, just big enough for two people.

One bed. For two people.

All my mountain man romance novel thoughts came rushing back, and my face heated up.

Surely, if I took the air mattress, Jackson would sleep on the floor. Right? Although that would make me feel like a jerk for taking the bed.

"I can't take your bed," I said decisively. "I'll sleep on the floor. I brought a blanket. And a pillow."

For the second time tonight, he looked at me like I'd lost my mind. "You're not sleeping on the floor. You'll freeze."

That implied *he* would sleep on the floor. And if he wanted to be the gentleman and offer me the air mattress, I decided I wouldn't say no. Especially since he was right—I'd be awake all night shivering if I slept on the floor.

It was too cold to even think about changing into anything else, and even if I had pajamas, I wouldn't consider wearing them in front of Jackson Harker. So I grabbed my new blanket and pillow, and did as he said. I slid under the blankets on the air mattress, still wearing his coat.

He didn't have a pillow. I should at least offer the one I bought to him. But before I could get a word out, he'd made himself at home on the air mattress beside me.

I froze, eyes wide, and afraid to turn over and face him. This was it. I was *living* in a mountain man romance novel, but with a functioning car and a man who was less grizzled and mountainy, and more dark and mysterious.

"Relax, Emily," he said with the hint of a laugh. "Your librarian's virtue is safe tonight."

I didn't know how I could feel simultaneously relieved and disappointed, but no way was I letting him think *that* was what was on my mind.

But I drew a total blank on witty retorts. "I *am* relaxed." I cringed as the words left my mouth.

"No wonder you're broke. If you sleep like that every night, I bet you spend all your money at a chiropractor's."

I wasn't giving him the dignity of a response this time, but I forced my body to relax, muscle by muscle. Which wasn't easy, considering the second I let my back curve, it hit Jackson's chest.

There was no way I was sleeping tonight. But at least I wouldn't freeze, considering the heat emanating from Jackson's body was enough to melt the polar ice caps.

When his head found the edge of the single pillow, I clenched every tendon in my neck to keep it from sliding sideways into him. His breath was hot against the back of my head, and I squeezed my eyes shut, trying not to think about it.

Or him.

To distract myself, I counted through the Dewey Decimal system the way other people might have counted sheep. *000 Generalities. 001 Knowledge. 002—*

Jackson shifted, lying face up so far as I could tell. My neck felt cold without his breath, but at least my head cleared a little.

And eventually, I fell asleep.

Only to wake up in the predawn light to find his arm slung around my waist and my back flush against his chest.

Chapter Ten

Marybeth

SATURDAY MORNING WAS A dazzle of sunlight on snow, as if spring had just been teasing us.

I sighed as I looked out the window of the house Gabe and I had recently moved into. For someone whose livelihood depended upon Christmas and winter in general, I should've been happy about the snow. Snow makes people think of winter, and winter makes them eager for Christmas. And Bent Creek Christmas was ready and waiting to fulfill their every holiday wish.

But like just about everyone else in the mountains, I was dying for a little warmth and sunlight.

Well, at least we got the sunlight. I smiled up at it wryly. Maybe this was a sign for me to move forward with my plans for summer at the shop. I had to cater to the summer resort guests, the people here for whitewater rafting and hiking. And I had a few things in mind that I hoped would mean I didn't have to ask Gabe for money to cover the shop's expenses.

He'd offered, and I was *this close* to desperate enough, but we'd just taken this major step in our relationship by moving in together, and the last thing I wanted was to feel indebted to him for my business. Things had been weird enough with our families—we didn't need anything else trying to pull us apart.

I finished opening the blinds to let in the sunlight and set about packing up the lunch I promised I'd deliver Gabe and his brothers at their old family ranch house. Fifteen minutes later, I had a cooler filled with ham and turkey sandwiches, cut fruit, tortilla chips, and cubes of cheese.

I threw on a coat, although the bright sun made it almost too warm for one, locked the door to the house, and brought the cooler to my trusty old Honda SUV. The snow was already melting off the windshield. I quickly brushed off what was left and made my way toward Quarter Mile Road.

With the move, I hadn't been out to the old ranch property in a while. I doubt they'd gotten much done on it yet, but Gabe's mood had been optimistic ever since he and Nick had cooked up this plan.

"Squatting?" I'd said skeptically when he first told me about it.

"Adverse possession," he corrected me. "According to state law, if a person lives in an abandoned property for five years, pays the taxes, and completes noticeable improvements to the property, he can claim it as long as the property owner doesn't tell him to leave during that time."

It was a good plan, but five years was a *long* time. Plenty of time for someone from Chestnut Moon, LLC to show up and kick Jackson out.

It was a longshot, but as Gabe said, it seemed like the only path, unless they could dig up some dirt on this company that owned the ranch and was buying up so many other properties in the area. So he paid the property taxes early in the hopes Chestnut Moon wouldn't notice, Jackson moved in, and this morning, they'd started on the first of a long list of chores to fix the place up.

I pulled into the driveway behind Gabe and Nick's trucks. Jackson must've been parked around back. I pulled out the cooler and shaded my eyes against the sunlight to better see the men up on the roof. They'd already swept off the snow and started pulling off the old shingles.

Gabe waved at me, and I held out the heavy cooler. He nodded. "Be down in a second."

"I'll put this inside," I yelled back.

Despite the sunlight, it was shadowy inside without any lights on. And cold. I didn't know how Jackson slept here at night, especially last night, without heat. And with no running water, I wasn't sure I wanted to know how he dealt with hygiene stuff. I liked camping, but only when there were toilets, sinks, and the weather was mild.

I set the cooler on the counter in the kitchen. A camping stove sat on top of the electric range, a dirty pan, spatula, and two used paper plates nearby. After checking on the amount of ice in the cooler, I retreated through the living room. At least Jackson had taken a moment to sweep the place out. I wasn't sure I wanted to know what it looked like before he moved in.

I absentmindedly reached down to move a blanket and a hair elastic out of the way.

A *hair elastic*?

I stared a moment at the ivory-colored stretchy band. And there were *two* dirty paper plates in the kitchen.

I wasn't sure whether to laugh or roll my eyes as I tossed the elastic toward the air mattress and blankets. Jackson had a girl stay over. In a cold house with no electricity or running water.

It was hard to blame her, though, whoever she was. After all, Larkin and I had both fallen for that magnetic Harker *something*.

"Hey," Gabe said as I walked out to the front porch. He might not have been a Harker in name or blood, but he shared that intense, devil-may-care personality trait with his stepbrothers. The one that made me want to melt against him and lose every sane thought in my head whenever I caught his gaze.

"Hey," I said, giving into my thoughts and molding myself against his body. "How's it going up there?" I leaned my head back to look up at him.

He gazed down at me with darkened eyes, and I wondered if I would ever get enough of him.

No, I decided. Never. And I liked it.

"Good." His hands clasped the small of my back. "Makes me glad the house isn't any bigger than it is."

"Roofing isn't in your future, I guess?"

Gabe laughed. "Definitely not. I'll take cattle over work like this any day. But it has to get done. That roof wasn't going to stand another winter."

"I put lunch in the kitchen."

"How domestic did you get?"

I wrinkled my forehead. "Deli ham and turkey and pre-sliced cheese and fruit. I would've added some of Larkin's cookies, but we kind of ate them all last night."

"Works for me. Thanks for bringing it."

"When do you think you'll be done?" I closed the shop at four on Saturdays, unless there was a rush of customers. "I was thinking I might make chili."

Gabe's brows arched in surprise. "I won't miss that, I promise." He leaned down and dropped a light kiss on my lips.

I smiled against his kiss, blissful in the idea that my entire day was taking care of my shop and making dinner for my boyfriend.

Except it wasn't.

I let out a frustrated groan, and Gabe pulled away. "I forgot I promised Luke I would work on the hen house." I'd lucked out and missed him when I went over there before, but he'd texted me and asked last night.

Gabe's jaw tightened. "You don't live there anymore."

"They're still my chickens. And he's still my family." I had less patience than ever for Luke's sideways comments about Gabe and my choice to be with him, but I also didn't love it when Gabe acted like I should cut Luke off entirely since I moved out of my family's home. Which seemed to happen more and more lately.

"We can build a chicken coop at our place," he said.

"That would be nice." I decided to leave it at that and tilted my head up to give him a kiss on the chin.

"Are you going to help us or make out all day?" Nick's voice called from up on the roof.

"I'm going with the second option," Gabe said, grinning ear to ear as he looked at me.

"Go help your brothers." *And don't act all put out when I need to help mine.* I shoved the irritated thought from my mind as I gently pushed Gabe away.

"I'll start the chili when I get home," he said.

I smiled at him as he made his way back around the house to the ladder. That was probably as close as I was going to get to him being okay with Luke.

And it wasn't like I could blame him. Learning that Luke had been in the car that had shot at his brothers and father—and Larkin—all those years ago had tilted both of our worlds sideways, for different reasons.

Gabe was still reckoning with being excluded from a secret that Nick and Jackson had carried, and I now saw my brother through different eyes.

But Luke was still my brother. Even if I dreaded going over there later.

Chapter Eleven

Jackson

I NEVER WANTED TO see another shingle as long as I lived.

Which was a tall order, considering we still had an entire roof to lay. And that I'd taken a job in construction.

I flexed my fingers against the steering wheel, stretching out the ache after hours of pulling off the old roof. We had to replace the decking on the back corner, and when Nick asked if it was leaking, I confessed I hadn't gone upstairs yet. *Too busy*, I'd said. Too chicken was the truth.

If I couldn't face the emotions lurking upstairs, I had to at least face the past in town. If I asked Emily to go to the hardware store for me again, I might as well hand over my name and everything it stood for.

Good or bad, I was a Harker. I could wear it like a badge or hide in the shadows. And I was doing enough hiding as it was.

I left the car in a no parking zone on Main Street. Bent Creek wasn't busy enough to warrant parking regulations anyway. And if I got back in that car, I was afraid I wouldn't get out again.

Flexing my sore hands, I made my way the few feet down the sidewalk to Town Square Hardware. I paused a second at the door, ran a hand through my hair, and went inside.

A bell tinkled over the door, and I fought the urge to cringe. If Old Man Lewis was here, he'd see me when I checked out. What difference did it make if he saw me now instead?

"Let me know if you need help," a male voice called from somewhere down the aisles. I couldn't find a face to put to the voice, but it sounded younger.

Melvin Lewis had to be pushing seventy by now. I released a breath. Maybe he wasn't here, and I'd gotten myself all hyped up over nothing.

There was a stack of dirty orange plastic baskets by the door. I grabbed one absentmindedly and ventured down the first aisle. I didn't need much. A drill for inside work, roofing nails, some lock de-icer, and a window scraper just in case the weather wasn't done with us yet. Nick and Gabe had already gotten the bigger stuff at the Home Depot an hour away from here.

I found it all without trouble. When I approached the single register, no one was there. I waited a moment, hand wrapped around the basket handles. Old Man Lewis still pinned up newspaper articles, just like he always had. That one about his kid winning the Bent Creek Fly Fishing Tournament twenty years ago was still there, flanked now by an obituary for some distant relative and an article titled "Town Square Hardware Wins 'Most Patriotic.'"

I glared at the fly fishing article, just as I'd done every time I came in here as a kid. No matter how many tournaments I'd entered back then, I never won. I was grown enough now to realize how pointless it was to be jealous of Lewis's kid winning, considering the guy was at least ten years older than me. But there wasn't any statute of limitations on childhood bitterness, so far as I knew.

After a few minutes, I realized no one was coming up here unless I said something. I cleared my throat. "Ready to check out," I called in the vague direction where I'd heard someone before.

"Dad, can you get the customer up front?" the same younger voice called.

Dad. A groan rose in my throat. Old Man Lewis was here. What were the odds he wouldn't remember me?

Zero, I decided. *Run*, my brain yelled.

I gritted my teeth against the instinct as Melvin Lewis shuffled up to the register from the bowels of the store.

"Afternoon," he said without looking up. He started pulling items from the basket. "You know we're running a two-for-one on these?" He held up the lock de-icer.

I could see every thought on his face when he finally looked up at me. Confusion. Recognition. Suspicion.

"Thanks, I only need one," I managed to say. "You know, with the weather . . ."

He eyed me a moment, narrowed blue eyes trying to decide if I was still a little punk thief. I pulled out my wallet, hoping to give him a signal that I actually had money to pay for this stuff.

His gaze lingered a few seconds more before he began totaling up my purchases on the register. We finished the rest of the transaction in silence, and as he bagged everything up, his kid stared at me from the newspaper clipping over Lewis's shoulder.

"Have a good day now," he said when he handed me the bags, like I was any old customer. Any regular person from Bent Creek.

"You too," I found myself saying back.

I felt like I'd just survived a life-threatening experience when I walked out of the hardware store. My heart beat hard, and my forehead was damp. I'd been prepared for the worst . . . and nothing had happened. It was just a store, but it seemed like I'd conquered some kind of mountain.

My phone buzzed as I pulled onto the street. I glanced at the cracked screen to see a text from my brother Ward. I could imagine what he was asking, from his cushy apartment in Los Angeles—had I really agreed to move into the old house?

The temperature had warmed, melting away most of last night's snow, and I rolled the window down as I headed back toward Quarter Mile Road. The wind on my face felt good, and my mind wandered away from Ward and back to this morning. I'd woken up with my arm slung around Emily's waist, and her shoulders pressed into my chest.

Let's just say it wasn't the worst way to start a day.

I hadn't moved, even as she stirred. It was freezing in the house, but she was like a heat lamp against me. She'd stiffened as she realized how we were arranged, but she didn't move either, not right away. And somehow we'd both fallen asleep again until the sun began to touch the sky.

I'd offered breakfast, but she'd shaken her head, saying she had to get to work. And with a hurried thank you, she'd gathered up her stuff and slid out the door into the snow.

She won't be back, I told myself the second my mind verged into imagining what we'd eat tonight, what we'd talk about, how we might wake up the same way. I'd already checked the weather, and the temperature was supposed to be mild tonight. Good for sleeping in a car.

It was for the best, anyway. I had too much to do to get tangled up with a girl, especially one as nice as Emily Foley. Although the fact that she'd stayed with me instead of going home to her parents made it pretty clear she wasn't who I'd thought she was.

I was trying to push my brain into thinking about the roof when the blue lights lit up behind me.

Chapter Twelve

Emily

I COULD TELL MOM knew before she said a word.

"Macadamia white chocolate chip. Your favorite," she said as she held out a little cellophane bag tied with a purple ribbon in the middle of the library's reading nook. The only patrons were another mother and daughter, but the mom was my age and the little girl was tiny and listening to her mother read board books.

I forced a smile as I took the cookies. If I was on the receiving end of a Carol Foley cookie delivery, that meant she knew I needed cheering up. My mom baked cookies weekly, and some time ago she'd made it her mission in life to gift them to anyone in town she thought needed a pick-me-up.

"Thank you." My mouth practically watered at the sight of the cookies. They *were* my favorite, and I'd made do with the world's tiniest can of soup for lunch. The cellophane crinkled under my fingers as I waited for the explanation—and questions—I knew would come.

"I ran into Keith Tarrant at the Snowshoe earlier. Your dad had a craving for their corn chowder. So I stopped in to the café, and

Keith was there, having a bite. We got to talking, and he apologized for evicting you and Anna. I didn't know what to say, Emily. Why didn't you tell me? Are you having money troubles? Do you need to come home?" The little crease on Mom's forehead deepened with her questions.

I hated worrying her even more than I hated the idea of Dad finding out. "I'm fine, Mom, I promise. Anna flaked on me. And I didn't say anything because, well . . . I've already got something lined up." I crossed my fingers behind my back like a little kid, as if that would absolve me from lying to my mother. I *had* talked to a potential roommate this morning, some woman Leo had met who was new to town. She looked as if she'd remember to pay rent maybe a quarter of the time, but at least I was making *some* progress.

But the crease in Mom's forehead smoothed, and she smiled as she wrapped a hand around my arm and squeezed. "I knew you'd have it figured out. Dad was sure you'd need to come home, but I reminded him our Emily was a smart cookie. But where are you staying? Are you sure you don't want our guest room?"

"Oh, no." I shook my head emphatically, pretending it was because I was on top of everything and not because I couldn't stand to see Dad's smug grin as I drug my sorry behind back through his door. "I'm staying with a friend right now. Just until I can get the new apartment situated. I'm having trouble deciding where." I smiled as if a plethora of affordable apartments was my biggest worry.

"Oh, good. Let me know if I can help you. You know I love a good home tour." Mom grinned, and all I wanted, more than anything, was to give her that. To be that daughter who had her life together and could take her on apartment tours and nail appointments and paint-and-sip classes, and all that other mom-and-daughter stuff my sister did with Mom when Mom visited her.

"Of course," I said, hoping I could make my words come true.

"Who are you staying with?"

"Oh, just a friend." I waved my hand like I had friends lined up to let me crash on their couches. I started walking back toward the front of the library, hoping Mom would drop the question.

But instead, she fell into step beside me, furrowing her brow. "Christa?"

I was pretty sure Christa Appleby hadn't said two words to me since kindergarten. "No. Um, it's . . . someone you don't know. Very well," I amended since Mom knew everyone in town.

Of course Mom wasn't going to let it drop there. I should've known better.

"Oh! Is it someone new to town? I'll have to meet her! What's her name?"

I winced inwardly. Saying Jackson Harker wasn't an option. Period. Mom would insist I come home, Dad's head would probably explode, and they would never leave me alone again.

Besides, I wasn't *really* staying with Jackson. That was just one night because it was snowing.

"Larkin Reyes," I said quickly.

"Oh, Larkin!" Mom clasped her hands together in delight. "She's such a sweet girl, and that little boy of hers is adorable. Have you tried one of her brownies? I'm proud to say I helped her perfect that recipe. And now she's selling them at the coffee shop!"

My heart took a nosedive into the deep end of the pool. And *this* was why lying got you nowhere. I should've known better. Bent Creek was too small for me to tell tales to my mother. She knew Larkin better than I thought she did. I could either backpedal and tell her the truth . . . or I could find Larkin—fast.

"Yeah, that's been really great for her!" I said with a smile pasted across my face as I ignored the voice screaming at me from the back of my head. It was a white lie, right? And it was better than facing Dad with the truth.

Mom went on about Larkin's baking before checking her watch and realizing she was late to meet Dad.

When she left, I slumped against the wall by the door. The job search class poster I'd hung up there crinkled behind my shoulder blades, and I let out a breath between my teeth.

So now I had to find Larkin, tell her what happened, and hope she agreed to go along with it even though we weren't more than acquaintances, really.

And even though I'd spent last night curled up with her boyfriend's brother.

Chapter Thirteen

Jackson

A CURSE ESCAPED MY mouth as I pulled over. At least I was still on the edge of town, nowhere close enough to Quarter Mile to give anyone suspicion about where I was staying. I didn't think I'd been speeding, but I hadn't exactly been paying attention to it either.

I kept the window down as I hoped for some young, new officer. Someone from out of town. Someone who had no idea who I was.

I bit back another curse when I saw who got out of the car. Officer Robert Scott. I gripped the steering wheel and schooled my expression into something neutral.

"License and registration," he said, and for half a second, I thought he might have forgotten who I was.

"My wallet's in my pocket."

His eyes narrowed. He knew exactly who I was. When he gave a quick nod, I reached back and pulled out my wallet. I handed my license to him and leaned over for the registration in the passenger seat.

"These addresses don't match." He peered at me over the sheet of paper, and all I could think about was that look he'd given me every time he thought he'd cornered me when I was a kid. Like a bear snagging a salmon in its teeth.

Lucky for me, I didn't have anything to hide these days—except my current address.

"I just moved back to town. Sir."

Scott grunted some kind of assent, eyes on me a second longer. I'd gone overboard with the *sir*. He folded up the registration paper. "You living by yourself over on Custer?"

"It's my brother's place."

He leveled that stare at me again, and I felt like a sixteen-year-old kid, trying to worm my way out of trouble. And at sixteen, the trouble I could've found myself in would've still had me locked up today.

"Which brother." His voice was flat, the question sounding like a statement.

"Gabe."

He eyed me a moment longer, then tapped a hand on my door. "Wait here."

"Can I ask why you pulled me over?" My question died in his wake as he retreated to his cruiser. I sighed and slammed my head back against the seat. He'd probably seen me coming out of the hardware store or leaving that no parking zone. I couldn't exist in this town without being under suspicion of something.

As I mentally paged through my adult life, adding up what would and wouldn't show up on Scott's screen when he ran my license, he reappeared at my door.

"That was illuminating. And expected." He held out my license and registration paper.

I pressed my mouth closed, silently fuming, as I took them from his hand.

"Must be a lucky day for you, Harker," he went on, thumbs tucked into his belt. "No outstanding warrants, the car belongs to you, and you even have insurance."

I swore he sounded disappointed when he said that. I opened my mouth to ask—again—why he'd pulled me over, but he spoke first.

"What are you doing here?" He rested a hand on the window frame.

"You pulled me over." My voice took an edge before I could smooth it over, honed from years of being on this man's radar. He didn't want us here, any of us. I was pretty sure the rest of the town felt the same way, despite what Nick and Gabe said. And out of all of us, *I* was the one Scott had it out for the most. I was the troublemaker. Then I was the one Pops had depended on—and Scott knew it. I would've found myself in charge of the whole business if it hadn't all gone south first. I wondered if he knew that too.

"What are you doing in Bent Creek?" Scott's words were sharper now, and the blood rushed to my ears.

"I don't know, building an empire of heroin and stolen cars." The bitterness seeped through my voice.

He leaned closer. "Are you trying to give me a reason to lock you up?"

I held his gaze. He wanted to cow me, and I'd never give him the satisfaction. "Funny, you never really needed one before."

Scott's jaw twitched. I'd touched a nerve with that half-truth. He'd always had plenty of reason back then, but nothing concrete. Nothing that would hold up.

"Say that again, and I'll ask you to step out of this car."

He'd *love* that. And like a teenager drunk on my own power, I was tempted to see how far I could push him. But I wasn't a kid anymore. I had more important things to do here in Bent Creek than waste time in a jail cell.

So I kept my mouth shut.

"That's what I thought." Scott straightened, a triumphant look crossing his face as he peered down at me.

I dug my nails into my palms to keep from doing what I *really* wanted to do. "Are we done here?"

He stood there a moment, purposefully dragging it out. He had no real reason to pull me over. I knew it, and he knew it.

Finally, he nodded. "I'm keeping an eye on you, Harker. You and your brothers."

"I'll let them know," I said lamely. I was over this. Over Scott, over the way this town tossed us out like trash, over all of it.

And suddenly, more than anything, I wanted to prove them wrong. They could like us or not, but we weren't going anywhere.

"You do that," Scott said. And after one last look at me, he turned and strode to his car.

I glared at him from my rearview mirror as I pulled away. I wouldn't have been surprised if he followed me, but instead, he turned around and headed back into town. I fumed for a solid five minutes, but the anger funneled quickly into that spark of hope I'd just felt.

I couldn't control how this town felt about me, but I could control the work I put into the house and the ranch. Piece by piece, I was going to put this place back together with Nick and Gabe's help. Make something of it—and myself.

It was going to be ours again, if it was the last thing I ever did. I'd bring it back to life, get the deed to it, make it profitable, and this town would eat its words.

The ambition and the lingering anger made me restless, like I could've jumped out and put the whole new roof on myself. The second I pulled into the driveway, I was ready to leap out of the car.

But I pulled up short when the drive around back was blocked by another car. One that looked familiar.

One that belonged to the woman standing on my porch right now.

Chapter Fourteen

Emily

I CLUTCHED THE PORCH post as Jackson emerged from his car, tall, rumpled, and with that lazy smile that sent my heart off on its very own marathon. If he was smiling, that meant he wouldn't turn me down.

I hoped.

He had a couple of bags in his hands as he approached. "I didn't expect to see you here again," he said.

"Yeah." The words died in my throat as he passed me, headed to the door. What was the right way to ask someone you barely knew if it was okay to crash at their place again? Especially when that someone was the last person in town you should be spending time with.

He unlocked the door and held it open silently. I slipped inside. I hadn't brought my bag in with me, not wanting to assume he'd say yes. He moved toward the kitchen, and I trailed behind him. Opening one of the bags, he pulled out a drill and some bits.

"You went to the hardware store?" I asked, too surprised to hesitate.

"Yeah," he said, turning around with a slight smile. "And I survived."

"I'm glad." I smiled back, glad that he was happy over such a small thing.

"So . . ." He braced his hands on the counter behind him and leaned back. "What brought you back, Shakespeare?"

My dumb heart did a flip over the silly nickname. "Well . . ." *Ask him.* "I feel like I kind of owe you for last night. I thought that maybe I could . . ." My brain latched on to the first thing that came to mind. "Clean out the gutters. Or something."

He stared at me a moment.

I could feel my face warming. "I mean, I saw the tarp on the roof and the shingles and I figured you were fixing the place up, so . . . The gutters are a mess."

And he was smiling again. "That's a nice offer, Shakespeare, but what I am supposed to do while you're working? Watch?"

I was pretty sure my face was tomato red at the thought of him watching me. "Um, I don't know. Make some more of those burgers?"

He laughed then, and it was such a warm, friendly sound that it made me relax. "So you're sending me to the kitchen while you do the manual labor. All right. You've got yourself a deal, Emily, but on two conditions."

I crossed my arms and smiled back at him. "What are those?"

"One, you only do one side of the house. And two, you'll have to be satisfied with grilled ham and cheese. I'm out of ground beef."

"Only one side? Are you sure?"

He shook his head like he couldn't believe me. "One side. If my brothers came by, I'd never hear the end of it."

"Ohhh . . . You're afraid of what people will think if they see me out there working alone." I stepped forward and poked him in the chest for emphasis. "I should've known you'd be old-fashioned like that."

He wrapped a hand around my pointing finger, and a million goose bumps broke out on my skin. "Maybe I am. I'm not going to apologize for it."

I didn't know what to say to that. Or anything. Because every nerve ending in my body was focused on the warm, calloused hand that covered mine. His dark eyes bored into me, and I had the distinct feeling he was trying to read my thoughts. And I couldn't make myself look away.

"Well, if you're going to work," he finally said. "You'd best get started while there's still daylight."

He let go of my hand, and I nodded. And when he gave me a wink, I stumbled backward and just about ran out the back door and around the corner of the house where I'd seen a ladder perched.

I pressed my hands to my hot face, grateful for the cool spring air. Why had I done that? I both hated and loved the way he made me feel like every part of me was on fire. And it was exactly why I'd come back here, even if I told myself it was only because I didn't want to sleep in my car.

I cringed at the honesty of my thoughts and tried to focus on what I'd just volunteered myself to do. I pulled a pair of thin winter gloves from my pockets, put them on, and got to work.

I'd made it almost to the end of one side of the house when I heard my name. Tossing a handful of rotted leaves to the ground, I spotted Jackson just below me.

"Food's ready," he said.

My stomach grumbled in response. "I'm almost done."

He waved a hand. "Leave it. It's almost dark anyway."

If I was going to gather up my courage and ask to stay here again, I wasn't about to leave work undone. "It'll take me five minutes," I said as I climbed down the ladder. I had to move it one last time to reach the end of the gutter.

"It's really not—Emily!"

He shouted my name as my foot slipped off the ladder about halfway down. My hands grabbed uselessly at the nearest rungs as I fell.

This is how my mother is going to find out I was lying to her. It was my only thought.

I hit the ground hard on my right foot. Pain shot through my ankle as it crumpled beneath me and I landed in a heap.

"I knew this was a bad idea. Are you all right? Emily?" Jackson squatted beside me, one hand on my arm.

And if I wasn't sucking in air at the throbbing pain in my ankle, I probably would have swooned at the all-encompassing concern he was showing. "Yes," I managed to get out. "I think I . . ." I pointed at my ankle as I ran out of breath.

Before I knew it, he was carefully holding my foot, pressing gently all around my ankle. His fingers were warm against my skin. I couldn't breathe, but now it wasn't because I'd just fallen off a ladder.

"I think you just twisted it." He sat back on his heels, clearly relieved he didn't have to bring me to the ER.

"Sorry." I didn't know why I was apologizing.

"Inside. Now." He stood up.

I started to push myself into a standing position when he reached down and—like I weighed nothing at all—scooped me up.

I was so surprised that I squeaked as I grabbed onto him, my hands instinctively reaching around the back of his neck.

"I can walk," I said, my voice sounding slightly frantic as he shifted my weight against his chest.

"Maybe, but we're not making it any worse."

I squeaked again as he tightened his hold around my back and my knees and began to walk.

"Relax, Shakespeare," he said. "I'm not going to drop you."

That wasn't what I was worried about. It was more like how I'd survive being this close to him with all of this . . . this *touching*, and not either explode, or do something really crazy and kiss him.

I squeezed my eyes shut to try to force that last embarrassing thought out of my mind.

Jackson must've mistaken it for fear, because when he spoke again, his voice was low and soothing. "Just let me help you."

I nodded, but I didn't dare open my eyes. If I did, I knew I'd be just inches from his face, and my traitorous body couldn't begin to handle that.

He carried me up the porch stairs and shifted slightly as he reached for the doorknob. I didn't open my eyes until he deposited me on the air mattress in the living room.

"Stay there," he said. "And don't move."

Chapter Fifteen

Jackson

I leaned forward and gripped the edges of the countertop as I forced my breathing to return to normal.

I didn't have to carry her in. I could've let her lean on my arm and hobble inside. It's what I would've done for anyone else.

But instead, some primal instinct had taken over, and I'd lifted her up and carried her inside like I had some kind of claim on her. I'd wanted the excuse to see how she felt in my arms, and now I was going to pay with the sweet torture of the memory of it.

I drew in a breath and straightened. Something about this girl made me feel like I was losing my mind, and yet instead of running away like I should have, I kept diving in headfirst.

I always did like to make things hard for myself.

Shaking my head at my own stupidity, I grabbed the two plates of sandwiches and chips and balanced a couple cans of Coke before heading back into the living room.

Emily reached up and took the Cokes from me without standing. I bit back a smile at the way she was agreeably staying put, like I'd told her. I handed her one of the plates before sitting down across from her on the floor.

"Thank you," she said.

"Sorry about the chips again. I'll get a vegetable or something next time." I took a swig of Coke to distract myself from the way Emily bit into her sandwich.

"I don't mind chips at all," she said after she swallowed. "Way better than carrot sticks. And this is possibly the best sandwich I've ever had."

A pleased sort of sensation buzzed through me. I'd never really had anyone appreciate my cooking before. It was nice that she noticed the effort I put into it.

The space stretched out between us as we ate. I didn't know what she was thinking, but my mind was a war between trying to forget how she'd felt in my arms and curiosity over why she'd come back here. At least it all made my run-in with Officer Scott a distant memory.

Emily broke the silence first. "You never told me why."

I raised my eyebrows. "Why . . . what?"

"What you're doing here, in this house." She gestured at the empty room with a potato chip. "With fixing the roof and everything."

"Right," I said, buying time to think. Could I trust her enough to tell her? Although if someone from Chestnut Moon came barreling in here to demand we leave, she'd be in just as much trouble as me. It wasn't fair to put her in that position without her knowing.

I set the remaining half of my sandwich down. "I'll tell you, but you have to keep it to yourself."

She nodded. "Of course."

I believed her. I didn't know why, but something in my gut recognized that Emily was someone who could keep a secret. "All right. I'm squatting." I went on to explain Gabe and Nick's plan to her.

"Five years is a long time without electricity or running water," she said, as if this whole idea made perfect sense to her.

"Yeah, I'm going to need to do something about that." Water was easier than electricity. There was a well. I just needed to find someone I could trust to deal with it.

"So." She looked around the living room as if she were seeing it again for the first time. "You think this place is worth all that effort?"

I knew she saw the water stains on the ceiling, the walls that needed a fresh coat of paint, and the dirt that gathered in the corners. But this house was more than that, even after everything that had happened. Something about facing Scott again made me realize I belonged here, in this house, on this land, more than I'd ever belonged anywhere else. I had a right to be here, no matter what anyone else thought. Pops might have messed up and Carson Noble took advantage of that, and the town might hate us, but that didn't change how I felt when I walked through the front door. "It is. It's complicated, but it's home."

Emily nodded, her eyes coming back to meet mine. "I understand. I'm glad I could help, even if it was just a little bit."

She didn't know how much those words warmed my heart. It was just some leaves in a gutter, but she meant what she said, and gratitude welled up inside me. I didn't know what to do with it, so I pointed at her foot. "Nearly helped yourself right to the hospital."

She smiled ruefully before her cheeks went pink, making those freckles stand out, and I knew she was thinking about how I'd carried her inside.

"Kind of like you did freshman year," she said.

I let out a snort. "How did you remember that?"

"Oh." Her face went darker. "Well, it was hard to forget you clomping around school on those crutches. How did you do that, anyway?"

"What, you didn't hear the rumors?" I nudged her leg with my foot.

"Which one, the motorcycle gang or jumping off the barn roof while high?"

I gave a rueful laugh. Both of those sounded exactly like what Bent Creek High School thought of me. "I was hunting with my pops. Fell out of a deer stand."

Emily looked at me a moment, and then she smiled. "That's so . . . normal. And klutzy."

I raised my eyebrows and nudged her leg again. "Are you calling me klutzy?"

"I am. Who falls out of a deer stand and breaks their leg?"

"It was *dark*. And besides, who falls off a ladder when they're halfway down?"

"Now, that's—" The chirp of a phone made her stop. Emily shifted sideways to pull one from her back pocket, and I secretly hated whoever had called her and interrupted our conversation. "It's my mom," she said in an unenthusiastic voice.

That was curious, but then again, the fact that she was here with me instead of at her parents' house—with heat, a shower, and a real oven—was curious too. I didn't ask her to elaborate before, but there was no denying the fact that I really wanted to know why.

"I have to take this or she'll just call again later."

"Go ahead." I stood up to make myself scarce. Gathering our plates, I shoved the last bites of my sandwich into my mouth and made my way to the kitchen.

But it was impossible not to hear her end of the conversation, especially in an otherwise silent house.

"No, you don't have to do that!" Emily's voice sounded alarmed. I peeked my head around the kitchen door to see her with her eyes wide and the phone pressed to her ear. "I mean, thank you, but Diego's asleep and I'm about ready to go to bed myself." She yawned for effect, and I grinned at the bad acting.

"How about if I just stop by tomorrow? Work is crazy right now." She slumped a little in what looked like relief at whatever her mom said next.

I leaned against the doorframe. It was useless to try to pretend I couldn't hear, so I might as well just wait it out here.

"Yeah, I'll tell her hi . . . Oh, okay." Emily squeezed her eyes closed for a second in what looked like pain. "I'll tell her that too . . . Yeah, she'll love it . . . Okay, thanks, Mom. I love you too . . . Bye."

She slammed her phone down on the air mattress, which didn't really have the effect she was probably looking for. Then she dropped her face into her hands.

"Everything okay?" I asked after a moment.

She dropped her hands and turned to look up at me. "It's my mom."

"Who . . . thinks you're staying with Larkin?" It wasn't hard to piece together from her end of the conversation after she mentioned Diego.

She winced. "Yeah. She wanted to stop by and bring Larkin a slice of cake."

That was weird, but asking about the cake would distract from what I really wanted to know. I crossed my arms and kept my eyes on her as I asked the question I was pretty sure she wouldn't want to answer.

"What's going on with you and your parents?"

Chapter Sixteen

Emily

THAT QUESTION WAS SOMETHING I didn't really want to answer. It was embarrassing and I couldn't imagine admitting it out loud.

"Come on," Jackson said, with a dangerous smile lifting half of his mouth. "I told you my secret. Only fair if you tell me yours."

If he kept looking at me like that, I'd probably confess every single thought in my head. In comparison, telling him the thing he wanted to hear wasn't really all that bad.

"There's not a lot to say," I started. "It's just that my dad's always been disappointed in my choice of a career. He thought I should have gone to some big name, out-of-state school, that I should've been a lawyer or some kind of business executive. But instead, I went to community college and then I got a master's in library science. Which pays hardly anything, but I love it, and he doesn't understand that at all."

"And if you stay there, you'll hear all about it," Jackson finished for me.

"Yeah. Along with a list of comparisons against my sister, who did everything right, according to Dad." The words came out more bitter than I'd intended, but if I was being honest, it was nice to say it out loud instead of keeping it all to myself, simmering deep down inside. "I'm sorry, that was a lot to lay on you."

"It's fine. If anyone gets messed up family dynamics, it's me." He pushed himself away from the doorframe and came back to the living room to join me.

"Thanks," I said as he sat down again.

"For listening? I kind of dragged it out of you."

"For letting me—" I stopped myself, realizing I hadn't exactly asked if I could stay here again.

But Jackson knew what I was going to say. It was clear from the way his lips curled up in a wicked grin. "For letting you crash here?"

"Is that okay?" He wouldn't say no . . . would he?

"It's fine, I guess. I'm not letting you walk out on that ankle any-way." He nodded at the foot I had extended out in front of me.

"Not *letting* me?" My ankle didn't hurt the way it had, but it was definitely swollen. I'd be better off staying put, but I wasn't about to let him think he could boss me around like that.

"You heard what I said." The man had no shame at all. "Just don't steal the entire pillow this time, okay?"

"I did not!" My entire body went warm as I remembered how I'd woken up that morning.

And I wondered if it would be the same tomorrow morning.

When the first rays of sunlight woke me, I didn't have to wonder any more.

It was chilly, but not nearly as cold as yesterday morning. And yet Jackson's arm was slung around my waist again, and my back was pressed against his chest.

My heart immediately started pounding too fast for this early in the morning. As much as the crazy part of my brain wanted me to close my eyes and enjoy the moment, I had to get up. I needed to find Larkin at the coffee shop before I went to work—and before my mom could find her.

I started to move, the cool air making me break out in goose bumps as I lifted the blanket, but Jackson's arm tightened around me.

I froze, heart beating wildly and my breath held. He was still asleep. He had to be, or he wouldn't have done that . . . right? A better question might've been why I kept putting myself in this situation. I was *not* the kind of girl who randomly woke up with a guy clinging to her.

Except maybe I was?

Biting my lip against the confusion—and the heady desire to pull the blanket back up and enjoy the confusing closeness with a man I was pretty sure I had a raging crush on—I extracted myself bit by bit from under Jackson's arm.

He shifted and turned over, and I waited a moment for him to wake up. He didn't though, and I wasn't sure if I was disappointed or relieved. I wanted to say something to him before I left—thank him, at least—but I also didn't want to get caught in conversation when I really needed to get to town early.

I silently put my shoes on, grateful that my ankle felt steady even if it was still a little puffy, and gathered my things before slipping silently out the door. It felt like a walk of shame, except nothing had happened, and no one was around to witness it.

The coffee shop was still dark when I drove by, so I went to the library first to change and brush my teeth. Then I took a quick walk down Main Street with the few other early risers.

Larkin had just flipped the sign from Closed to Open when I got there.

"Hey," she said brightly. "How's it going? Did you find an apartment?"

"So that's why you're giving stuff away." Marybeth stood nearby, already sipping on a cup of coffee from a Mountain Roasters travel mug. "I forgot to send you that list. I've been really busy, but I promise I will soon."

"Sure, that's fine." I gave her a smile as I tried to recover from the fact that she was here too. What I had to ask Larkin was awkward enough; it was even worse to have to do it with someone else listening in. I turned back to Larkin, hoping this would go easier than how I'd made it out in my mind. "Um, no apartment yet. But soon. I'm still looking for a roommate, in case you know anyone."

"Wasn't Flannery looking for a place?" Marybeth asked Larkin. A little flame of hope sparked. Maybe it was a good thing she was here.

"Yeah, I think so. But she has the baby . . ." Larkin looked at me.

"That's fine with me. I like babies." I hadn't ever considered a roommate with kids, but it honestly didn't matter. I needed an apartment, sooner rather than later.

"She comes in a lot. I'll ask her next time I see her," Larkin replied. "You want a coffee?"

I found myself nodding even though I really shouldn't be spending the money. We had a little coffeepot in the library breakroom, and I'd been making do with that. I followed Larkin to the counter, Marybeth at my side.

"I bet you're ready to move out from your mom and dad's," Larkin said conversationally as she poured the coffee into a large cup.

"Oh, well . . ." I shifted from one foot to the other and adjusted my purse as I tried to figure out what to tell her. "I'm . . . not really staying there right now."

"Sorry, I thought you said you were." Larkin slid the coffee toward me, and I wrapped my hands around the cup.

"Yeah, I know. I'm, um, actually staying with a friend." Jackson counted as a friend, sort of. I didn't know what else to call him, anyway. "But, so . . . my mom doesn't know that."

Larkin's eyebrows went up and she leaned against the counter on her elbows. "A guy," she said, after a moment had passed and I hadn't elaborated. "You're staying with a guy, and you don't want her to know."

"Well . . . um . . . yeah." It wasn't a lie. At least she didn't ask me who.

"A boyfriend?" Marybeth asked.

"No," I said a little too fast.

Curiosity colored Marybeth's face, and I could tell she was dying to know who.

"Just a friend," I added. "It's temporary. *Very* temporary."

Marybeth nodded slowly.

"So . . ." I turned back to Larkin. "My mom kind of thinks I'm staying with you. Because you offered, and it was all I could think of when she asked."

Larkin didn't say anything, but she definitely looked surprised.

Of course she was. She barely knew me, and here I was weaving her into my lies. "I'm sorry—I shouldn't have said that. But it just came out, and now it's what she thinks. And so if she asks you . . ." I couldn't bring myself to ask her to cover for me.

But Larkin shook her head. "Don't worry about it. For all she'll know, you're sleeping on my couch every night."

"Oh, *thank* you!" I wanted to collapse on the floor in relief. "I promise it won't be for very long. And I'll pay you back. Free babysitting, or I'm sure I can weed some books at the library for Diego, or—"

"Emily." Larkin reached across the counter and laid a hand on my arm. "It's okay. I've done this kind of thing a million times for Marybeth."

"Are you serious? You're the one I always had to cover for!" Marybeth shot back, but she was smiling.

Larkin laughed, and I did too, just a little. It felt nice to be included in their friendship, even if it felt like I'd pushed my way into it. I took a sip of my coffee and relished the moment.

"I can't believe you're drinking that black," Marybeth said.

"Marybeth likes to taste sugar instead of coffee," Larkin said.

"Can you believe Gabe questioned the amount of creamer I have in the fridge?" Marybeth rolled her eyes, but she was smiling.

I smiled too as I took another sip, and I kind of wished I could stand here forever, feeling like I was just another friend of theirs.

Chapter Seventeen

Marybeth

There was *no* way that sweet, quiet Emily Foley was the girl who left that hair elastic behind at the old Harker house.

My mind could hardly wrap itself around the idea. For one, she and Jackson were night and day. Two, she was so *nice*. Three, plenty of girls had ivory-colored hair elastics. Four . . .

Just, *no*. My mind was so eager to find something else to distract it besides my impending stop at my own family's ranch, that it had latched on to the wildest possibility.

Still . . . they had been in the same class in school, both a year ahead of Larkin and me. Emily confessed to staying with a guy. It was entirely possible, as farfetched as it was.

I stopped my car in front of the garage, next to trucks of every make and model belonging to the ranch hands, and took a moment to psych myself up. All I had to do was check on the repairs I'd made to the henhouse. And with any luck, I'd avoid my brother. If I could get through this, I could go home and spend the evening cuddling with

Gabe and watching TV. And nothing sounded better than that right now.

I shoved my keys into my pocket as I closed the car door. The ground was still damp from the snow that had melted yesterday, and I was glad I wore boots. Avoiding the house, I walked past it and down to where I kept my chickens. If Gabe was serious about us building a chicken coop, I could move all my hens over to our place.

Luke would hate that.

I walked around the coop, testing the new wire I'd put up and the hinges I'd fixed on the henhouse. Everything seemed to work fine, and the chickens looked happy to see me.

"Hey, girls," I said, watching them strut around. The chickens always lifted my spirits, and I stood there a moment, letting myself enjoy watching them.

"They miss you." Luke's voice sounded from behind me.

I turned around to see him standing there, hands in his pockets. A few of the men who worked for him walked by in the distance, likely headed to dinner. It was a busy season in ranching, and Luke's appearance showed it, from the weariness etched across his face to the dirt streaked across his jeans and old plaid shirt.

"I miss them." I glanced at the chickens, wishing I could see them every day. But that would mean coming here and listening to Luke.

He sighed and toed the ground with his boot. "Look, I know you're annoyed with me. About everything."

That was an understatement.

"Even though you've pretended not to be sometimes."

I closed my eyes, then opened them again and stepped outside the coop. "You're right," I said quietly, crossing my arms. His hazel eyes—the same color as mine—looked the same. Kind, a little sorrowful, familiar. And his hair still curled at the ends, like it always had.

When I looked at him, I still had a hard time believing he lied to me for so long. And believing what he did all those years ago. Even if he wasn't the one with the gun, he was still *there*. He was part of that awful night that could have taken my best friend's life.

It was hard to rectify all of that with the Luke I knew. The big brother. The man who broke into pieces when he lost his wife. The one I took care of.

And then add to that his constant unwanted opinions about my relationship, and it was no wonder that it was easier to stay away.

"Marybeth." He pulled off his hat and rubbed a hand across the back of his head. "Can't we call a truce?"

"To what? I'm not fighting with you. I'm just trying to . . . figure everything out."

He sighed again and tapped his hat against the side of his leg. "I talked to Dad yesterday. He's worried about you."

I dug my fingers into my palms. The last thing I needed was concern from more family members. I never told Dad directly about moving in with Gabe. I'd told Mom, who'd been hesitant, but understanding. Having her break the news to him was easier.

"I'm fine. I hope you told him that. The store is good, the new house is great, and I'm happy."

Luke's jaw worked, like he was holding back something he really wanted to say. "I talked to Wilder too. He's engaged."

That was something new. Wilder was the second oldest in our family, twin to Drake. They'd both moved to Florida, near Mom and Dad, to help Dad manage his businesses. Neither one had been back here in years. They touched base through text now and then, busy with their own lives. This was the first I'd heard of a girlfriend, much less a fiancée.

"Wow," I said. "That's big."

"Yeah. Guess we'll be making a trip to Florida."

I cringed inside at the thought of dealing with all of my family at a wedding. Not when things were so weird between me and Luke. I could just imagine how strained it would be with everyone else. And was I supposed to bring Gabe as a date? Or leave him here?

Suddenly, I had a throbbing headache.

I pressed two fingers to my forehead. "I should go."

Luke stepped aside as I hurried by, ready for the quiet sanctuary of my Honda.

"Hey, Marybeth," he called when I was halfway to my car.

I stopped and turned around, keys in my hand.

"I heard a rumor that Jackson Harker's back in town now. You seen him around?"

My jaw clenched. I had no interest in being my brother's spy, but I wasn't the liar in this family. "Yeah, I have."

His lips flattened. "Do you know why?"

"You'll have to ask him." I spun on my heel and walked as fast as I could to my car as my head pounded.

By the time I sat down and closed the door, I felt sick to my stomach too. All I wanted was for history to stay in the past. But from that look on Luke's face, I had the awful feeling that it wouldn't.

Chapter Eighteen

Jackson

The Pine Street Bar was a dose of comfortable familiarity in a town where most of the familiar felt like it was about to strangle me.

Not that I was ever old enough to drink here before I left town, but I'd spent more than one night in this bar with Pops, throwing back Cokes while sneaking an occasional sip of beer when he wasn't looking. The owner, Mr. Rosso, always seemed to look the other way when I was in here. The place still had those booths with the cracked leather seating, the dim lighting, and a wooden bar so dark it was practically black.

It was busy when I walked in the door, busy enough that no one noticed me as I made my way to the bar. I was early to meet Nick, so I settled onto one of the few empty barstools. I didn't recognize the guy next to me, which was nice for a change. He nodded and went right back to flirting with the girl beside him.

"Jackson Harker." William Rosso stood behind the bar. He was Pops' age, and his hair was entirely gray now.

It made me wonder if Pops had gone gray yet.

"Mr. Rosso, good to see you." I held out a hand, and he shook it. It was the first handshake I'd had in this town, I realized.

"No *mister*. I feel old enough as it is. It's nice to see you. Nick and Gabe have been in a few times. Didn't know you were back here too."

"I guess I am." I didn't elaborate, but it was nice to be openly welcomed by someone in Bent Creek. Although, if I were honest, no one had been outright rude—except Officer Scott. But I could've predicted that. I couldn't have predicted everyone else being so ambivalent, and sometimes even nice.

"What're you having?"

I picked something dark and local and sipped on it as I scrolled through my phone and waited for Nick. I checked the door every couple of minutes, impatient for him to get here. I had things to do.

Like buy some vegetables.

I didn't dare finish that thought. The second I started hoping for Emily to come back, that would be when she'd find a place that was more comfortable. I needed to get the water situation straightened out soon.

But for myself, not for her, of course. I was getting tired of taking showers in the construction site trailer.

"So it's true," a loud, male voice said from behind me.

I put my phone in my pocket and turned around on the barstool. And found the other person in town guaranteed to give me a hostile welcome.

Luke Noble.

I sat there, half on and half off the barstool, waiting for him to finish his thought. I was bound to run into him at some point. He was the only one of the Nobles still here, except for Marybeth, Nick had told me. And not only was he pissed about his sister and Gabe, he wasn't happy at all to see any of us back in town.

Well, I wasn't thrilled to see him either.

"Answer a question for me, Harker. Why are you all slithering back here after so long?"

His choice of words, slurred from whatever he'd been drinking, lit a flame somewhere deep down, one that been smoldering for years. I stood up and shoved my hands into my pockets like his presence bored me. "What's it to you?"

Luke gave a short laugh. "Just answer the question."

I glanced behind me, keeping up the pretense of boredom. Rosso had paused his work behind the far end of the bar to watch us, but aside from the guy next to me, no one else paid us a lick of attention.

"I heard it would annoy the crap out of you, so I ran back as fast as I could." My voice matched my posture.

His eyes narrowed. "You're not welcome here."

I raised an eyebrow. "That's news to me," I lied. Jerking a thumb over my shoulder, I added, "Rosso was happy to see me."

"Because he's still afraid of your old man."

His words were like a dull knife, digging in over and over. I dropped my hands from my pockets, suddenly exhausted from it all. "You won, Noble. Remember? Now go away." I turned back to my barstool, grabbed my beer, and pulled my phone out.

There was a text from Nick. *Sorry, got caught up with Larkin and Diego. Tomorrow?* The second I finished reading it, a hand gripped my shoulder. I whipped around, beer forgotten, and shook Luke off.

"I wasn't done talking to you." His voice was loud, too loud. More people were watching now.

I forgot to pretend I was bored. I forgot about being tired. My gaze bored into his. "You've got a problem with my brother, you take it up with him."

He laughed, and half the bar went silent. A couple of guys I didn't recognize and another one I barely remembered from high school drew in behind him.

"I've got a problem with *all* of you. There's not a soul in this town who doesn't remember what kind of mess your family brought here."

It was my turn to laugh. Then I took a step forward. "That's one hell of an accusation coming from you." I dropped my voice just low enough for him to hear. "You and your brothers played like you were above it all, but I know you weren't. I know exactly how your family made money. I knew those guys you were riding with that night you came by. Remember that night?"

He swallowed, and I knew I'd hit a sore spot. That was enough. I knew it was, but I couldn't resist pushing further.

"Get out of here, Luke. Unless you're looking to find yourself in the hospital again."

His mouth curled into a sneer. "That was two on one, in case you forgot. You don't have your big brother here to help you now."

My jaw clenched, and all I wanted to do was hit him right in his smug face. Hot anger overflowed like a volcano, and I had to grip my hands to keep from lashing out. The last time I did this, with some stranger at a bar a couple hours north of here, I found myself with a hundred and twenty days in county jail. Acting on impulse would be stupid.

But I sized him up anyway as years of hate festered inside. "And you don't have your daddy to run to."

"Neither do you, but I bet they've got a nice cell all ready for you right next to his."

I stepped closer, and Rosso appeared out of nowhere.

"Outside, both of you," he growled.

"That's fine with me. Wouldn't want to mess up your bar." I kept my eyes on Luke as I spoke.

His gaze cut to Rosso. Then he nodded, and as the guys he must have come with whooped it up good, he stalked out the door.

"I owe you for that beer," I called to Rosso as I strode after Luke.

The sun had gone down, and the flickering streetlights someone must've thought looked quaint had flickered on. People were out, enjoying the spring temperatures, some locals, some tourists. But I barely noticed any of them as I watched Luke.

"What are you waiting for?" he said, circling around in front of me. "You too chicken to come after me?"

He was goading me into starting it. I knew that, but logic was something I was having a hard time hanging on to. He laughed, and I lost my grasp on it entirely. My brain shut down, and all I saw was my fist smashing into his face.

An arc of satisfying pain shot up my arm. He stumbled backward, hand to his nose, as the guys with him egged him on.

"What are *you* waiting for?" I turned his question back around on him.

He shot forward. I dodged his right fist, but realized too late it was a fake-out as his left got me in the stomach.

Breath wheezed from my lungs as I bent forward. He was a better fighter now. Better than when Nick and I put him down after he'd ridden up with those drug smugglers and shot at us all those years ago.

Stand up, Pops' voice sounded from somewhere deep in the back of my mind. *Fight like you know what your last name is, boy.*

Luke wasn't ready for me when I slammed into him. I knocked him straight down to the concrete and immediately rammed a blow to the side of his face.

"Jackson!" a woman's voice called my name just as Luke's fist connected with my cheekbone.

Stars exploded behind my eyes, and I had the weirdest thought that the woman was Emily.

"Did anyone call the police?" another voice said from somewhere far away.

Luke had taken advantage of the moment and rolled me over. I blocked another blow, then lashed out as fast as I could. I hit his jaw just as someone pulled him off me.

I jumped up immediately, my head spinning but my mind clear. Luke Noble was begging for a beating, and I was going to give it to him if it was the last thing I did.

"Let go!" he roared as his friends grabbed him by the arms.

All the better for me. I darted forward, ready to bloody up his face a little more, when Emily leaped in front of me.

Chapter Nineteen

Emily

The Pine Street Bar wasn't on my way to my car, but like everyone else who was out nearby, the commotion drew my attention.

I'd figured it was some tourists making a racket. It happened sometimes, a side effect of being a town that survived on people finding their way here from the nearby ski resorts. I crossed the road to see what was going on, and by then a small crowd had formed.

I reached the edge of it, then stopped cold. My stomach lurched as I realized what was happening. Jackson was doubled over, and faster than my mind could work, he straightened and ran right into Luke Noble.

I had to do something. But what? I felt sick as I yanked my phone from my pocket. I could take a picture faster than I could type, so I snapped one and then wrote out a quick text to Marybeth. *Help.*

I looked up just as Jackson punched Luke, and a ragged scream tore itself from my throat. "Jackson!"

He paused for a second, like he heard me. But his attention went right back to Luke, and I couldn't wait for Marybeth or anyone else. I moved forward just as someone behind me asked if anyone had called the police.

If the police came, my parents would find out. They'd know I was here, that I was trying to break up the fight, and they'd ask a hundred questions.

But right then, I didn't care at all. All that mattered was getting Jackson out of this before he got hurt—or before he hurt Luke.

The second I got there, a couple of guys yanked Luke off Jackson and dragged him backward. Jackson leaped up, oblivious to the trickle of blood on his cheek. He took one step toward Luke, and I didn't hesitate.

I stepped right in front of him. "Jackson." He glanced at me, confused, then looked back up toward Luke. I put a hand out toward his chest. "Stop!"

His eyes found mine again, but it felt like he didn't really see me. He went to step around me, but someone pulled him backward. Relief flooded my bones as I recognized the owner of the bar.

"That's enough," Mr. Rosso said, his voice low as he spoke to Jackson.

Jackson pulled against him, but Mr. Rosso held tight. "He was asking for it." Jackson's voice was ragged as his gaze still sought out Luke.

"I know," Mr. Rosso said. "You gotta let it go right now. The cops are on their way."

Jackson went still, and finally, it seemed as if he saw me. "Emily?"

Mr. Rosso glanced at me. "Are you taking responsibility for him?"

Was I? I nodded before I could think it through. "I'll get him home."

"Go on, then." He let go of Jackson, who stumbled a little.

I grabbed hold of his arm as Mr. Rosso watched us, probably to make sure Jackson didn't lurch around to go running after Luke.

Jackson didn't say a word as I led him across the street. An old SUV screeched to a stop behind us, blocking the turn from Main onto Pine Street. The door slammed, and Marybeth jumped out. "What the hell, Luke?" The anger in her voice could've stopped a hundred men in their tracks.

Jackson laughed a little before grimacing. "That hurts."

"I bet it does. What were you thinking?"

"I wasn't." He paused as we reached my car. "I'm parked over by the bar."

I shook my head and unlocked the doors. "I'll drive you. Mr. Rosso won't forgive me if I let you go back there. You can get your car tomorrow."

He hesitated, glancing back toward the bar. Blue lights began to reflect off the darkened buildings, and that seemed to make up his mind. We were driving away as the cruiser pulled up behind Marybeth's SUV.

"You didn't have to rescue me," he said, wincing as he touched his cheek. "I can take care of myself."

I handed him a tissue and hoped he had a first-aid kit back at the old house as I pondered how to respond. I *didn't* have to step in. But I couldn't have walked away.

Not from him.

Terrified of what that meant, I left his statement unanswered and decided to ask him a question instead. "So what was that all about?"

Chapter Twenty

Marybeth

I was fuming.

And Gabe didn't get it.

"Why didn't you call me?" he demanded the second I walked in the door after making sure my brother's ranch hands were taking him home. Gabe had his keys and phone in one hand, and I knew he was headed out to check on Jackson.

I rubbed a hand over my exhausted forehead. "I'd just gotten to my car when I got the text. I didn't have time to call you. I had to go after Luke."

"You don't have to be responsible for him. Not anymore."

I sucked in my cheeks and then let them go. "I *know* that, but I didn't stop being his sister just because I moved in with you."

He watched me a moment, then dropped his phone and keys onto the counter before holding out his arms. "I'm sorry. I didn't mean it like that."

I eyed his open arms, trying to hang on to my anger, but really only wanting someone to hold me. I closed my eyes and fell into him, my face pressed against his chest. One of his arms wrapped around me, while the other rested against the back of my neck. "I don't understand why he can't just let it go."

"I don't either," Gabe said, his voice a rumble against my ear. "And I get it, you know."

I felt so stupid. Of course he understood. Nick was the same way, and Gabe was constantly having to check him.

I leaned back and looked up at him. I loved him *so* much that sometimes it hurt to think about. "Do you think it'll ever get easier?" I asked in a quiet voice.

"I hope so," he said. "But I don't know."

I searched his face, wondering if he was thinking the same thing I was. I didn't dare say it out loud, but it was there, lurking in the back of my mind.

What if what we had wasn't strong enough to survive the years of hatred between our families?

I buried my face in his chest again, and he tightened his grip around me. I pushed the awful thought away, choosing instead to focus on this moment.

"I need to check on Jackson." Gabe pressed a kiss to the top of my head.

I nodded and stepped back. "Go. Tell Emily I said thank you."

"Emily?" He looked confused, but he'd find out soon enough. I still couldn't believe I was right about her and Jackson.

I smiled instead of answering him.

"Will you be all right?" he asked.

I nodded. I might not be tomorrow when I'd have to face a sober Luke, but for right now, I was okay. "Come back soon."

He smiled at me, and everything else that worried me felt a little less important. "I will. I promise."

Chapter Twenty-one

Jackson

I HAD TO HAND it to Gabe. If he was surprised to see Emily here, pressing a cotton ball dipped in peroxide to my face on the front porch, he didn't show it.

"Doesn't look like anything's broken," he said as he leaned against one of the posts.

"I would've taken care of that for Noble if Rosso hadn't stepped in," I growled.

Emily frowned, but she didn't say anything as she pulled the cotton ball away. I'd procrastinated on her question in the car in order to text Gabe.

"That wasn't a smart move," Gabe said.

"I didn't start it. But I wasn't going to back down."

Emily held out a bandage, and I held still while she applied it to my cheekbone. The brush of her fingers against my skin made every pain in my body fade into the background. "And you didn't have to come here. I just wanted to let you know."

"Of course I was going to come. You don't send me a text like that and expect anything else." Gabe sounded annoyed with me, and that was the last thing I wanted. I messaged him because he was the voice of reason. Nick would've come, guns blazing, and ready to take the fight over to Noble's ranch.

And that wasn't what I wanted either.

Emily packed up the first-aid kit Gabe had the foresight to bring the first day we worked on the roof. I forced myself to stand up, grimacing at the pain.

"So how do we deal with this? I can't be looking over my shoulder every five minutes, not if we want to get this place fixed up." I gestured at the house. "Can't you talk to your girlfriend?"

"Marybeth's got enough to deal with," he said shortly.

That was interesting, but if she couldn't keep her brother reined in, it didn't concern me. "Then what? He doesn't want me—or any of us—here. He made that perfectly clear."

"I know." Gabe rubbed a hand over his face. "Believe me, I know." He sighed. "You stay focused on the house, and let me see what I can do. And maybe stay out of the bars for now."

I kept silent at the fact that it was Nick's idea to meet up there anyway. "The cops were there. Pulled up as we left."

Gabe frowned slightly. "Shouldn't be a big deal unless Noble decides to press charges, and you didn't hurt him enough for that. Right?"

"Yeah, but . . ." I hadn't told him or Nick about getting pulled over. "I'm already on their radar. Scott made sure to let me know that the other day."

"Robert Scott?" Gabe asked.

"The one and only. He pulled me over for no reason to tell me that."

Gabe swore under his breath. "Just stay out of trouble, okay? I'll see what I can do."

"All right. Thanks, Gabe."

He stepped forward and gave me a clap on the back. "By the way, Emily, Marybeth told me to relay her thanks to you."

"Okay. I'm glad it helped," Emily said softly.

I sucked my breath in through my teeth as I sat back down on the steps. After a moment, when Gabe's car had disappeared down the road, Emily sat next to me.

"You sent for Marybeth to clean up after her brother?" I asked.

She nodded. "I thought she'd want to know." She paused. "Gabe seems nice. I never really talked to him much before."

"Yeah, he's the best one of us." If I'd been more like him, I'd have been in a better place in my life by now. Probably with loads of money to throw at fixing up this house and making Chestnut Moon an offer they couldn't turn down.

Emily's arm bumped mine as she set her hand down on the porch between us. I glanced at her. She was a pretty face, but was there was so much more to her than that. She was smart, stubborn, and had a heart of gold. And for whatever reason, that heart seemed to like me enough to step into a fight for my sake.

"You could've gotten hurt," I said. "Back at the bar."

She swallowed. "I didn't really think about that. I just wanted it to stop. Besides, those guys were holding Luke back."

Still, it was more than she owed me. That was for sure. "And then you took me back here and fixed me up."

"Of course I did." She sounded like there was no other option. "Why?"

The breeze caught the ends of her hair, sending them flying while she held my gaze. Those eyes were almost too much for me, and right now I thought I saw something reflected in the moonlight. Some kind of innocent hunger.

I gritted my teeth against the desire that suddenly raged through me. I didn't care that it hurt to breathe or that my face felt like it had run into a truck. All I wanted to do was pin Emily against one of these porch posts and kiss her until I was all she ever thought about.

She looked away then, the moment collapsed, and I drew air into my screaming lungs.

"You didn't say you got pulled over." Her voice was breathy, like she might have been thinking the same things I was.

I forced myself to focus on her words, and not on the images that were waiting at the edges of my mind. "Yeah."

"What happened?"

I dared to sneak a glance at her. She looked genuinely interested—and concerned. And I figured if she was crazy enough to haul me away from a fight and stay here, I at least owed her the truth.

So she could decide if she'd had enough of the mess that came with the Harkers, and get out of here before it consumed her too.

"It was Officer Scott. You know him?" It was a dumb question. Of course she did. She grew up here too, after all.

She nodded. "He used to play poker with my dad. Every Thursday night when I was a kid."

It figured. "I knew him back then too, but it was because he was usually the one calling my dad or booking me into the county juvenile detention."

Nothing changed on Emily's face. I hadn't scared her away yet. Then again, I hadn't told anything she wouldn't have already known—or guessed.

"So there's a lot of history between you two," she said.

"Yeah." I paused for a moment, letting the sounds of the evening take over. It was comforting, like I could close my eyes and feel like a little kid again. Back before anything bad had happened. Before I'd lost my mom and Katrina, before Pops's life had become mine. Before I lost him too, and I spent the years since floundering with no goal except surviving to the next day. And even that was sometimes questionable.

"Back in the car, you asked what happened between me and Luke," I said.

"Well, I mean, I know what everyone does. Your family never got along with the Nobles. Mr. Noble was the one who pointed the authorities toward your dad, and . . ."

"He went to prison and we all left?" I filled it in for her. She nodded, and I turned, trying to make myself more comfortable. It was a pointless endeavor, so I gave up and stayed put. Instead, I stared out at the giant evergreen that had flanked the front driveway ever since before I could remember.

"What happened tonight?" she asked carefully, as if she didn't want to disturb me.

"Nothing I shouldn't have expected. Luke's mad about his sister and Gabe, and he needed to take it out on someone. He brought up the past, acting like his family was entirely law-abiding and too good to stoop to the kind of work my father—and I—did." I shifted my gaze toward her to see if she understood.

She took in a deep breath and let it out. "Drugs? There were rumors," she said as if she had to explain away the truth.

"It was more than rumors." I decided to leave it at that. She didn't need to know every ugly detail. "Pops wasn't always the most careful. And the Nobles were better at keeping it separate from everything. If the cops knew, they were paid off, but I wouldn't be surprised if they didn't know. Carson Noble kept their reputation untarnished. He was good—really good—at that. He came off as the hero, and our name was dragged through the mud."

Emily's eyes were round. "I didn't know that about them."

I let out a wry laugh. "No one does. According to Gabe, even Marybeth didn't know the whole of it until recently."

"Wow. I have issues with my dad, but that's a whole other level of issues. And Luke's not thrilled any of you are back here?"

I nodded. "Too bad for him, because we aren't going anywhere. We're getting this ranch back if it kills me." And I meant it. This place gave me purpose, a reason. It was more than I'd had for years.

"And the police aren't happy about it either," she added.

"You scared away yet?" I watched her from the corner of my eye.

Emily laughed, and the sound made me smile. "It takes a lot more than some stuff that happened more than ten years ago to scare me away."

It was like she knew exactly the right words to say.

"But what you did back then," she said, her voice a little more guarded. "Is that in the past?"

I turned and made sure I was looking her in the eye when I spoke, because I wanted her to know I was telling her the truth. "When I worked for my father, yes. I haven't taken the easy road since then, you should know that. There's stuff I've done . . . some of it was dangerous, all of it was stupid. But since I've come back here, I don't know—it's like this place has given me something new and good to do with my life. I can't explain it, but it makes me feel like I can be more than I ever was."

She held my gaze a moment and then nodded. "Okay."

And it was like something in my soul scarred over with that one little word. "Okay."

Then I dared to lay my hand on top of hers as we sat there in silence and let the noises of the Montana spring night do the rest of the talking.

Chapter Twenty-two

Marybeth

It was NOT Emily! No way!

I grinned at Larkin's text. With everything that had happened the night before, it was nice just to gossip with my best friend.

I swear it was. She texted me and then she took him home! I typed back.

OMG. No. I won't believe it till I see it.

The bell above the door to my shop rang as I finished another text to Larkin. *Go by the ranch tonight. Bet you she's there.*

When I looked up, ready—and slightly desperate—for a customer, I found my brother instead. My good mood drowned fast.

"Hey," he said.

"You look awful." I set my phone down and went around the counter to see him better. "He got you pretty good. Who cleaned this up? It's a mess." I reached up to stretch out a crooked Band-Aid beneath his right eye, which was ringed in blue and black bruising.

He swatted my hand away.

"Did it myself," he said.

"Figures." I stepped back and dropped my hand to my hip. "Did you come to apologize for acting like a jackass?"

He scowled at me. "I didn't do anything wrong."

I was pretty sure my mouth fell open. "You started a *bar fight*, Luke. I had to talk to the police for you, tell them you were too drunk to know better and that you'd be better off sleeping it off at home instead of a jail cell."

"Fine," he muttered. "Thanks for that. I'm setting the police straight today, by the way. Harker's the one they should've picked up last night. He threw the first punch."

I shook my head, already over this conversation. "According to Mr. Rosso, you wouldn't leave him alone. You kept messing with him and—"

"Am I the *only* one in this town who sees a problem with them coming back here?" Luke slammed a hand on my counter, and I jumped.

Glaring at him, I stepped forward again. He was nearly a foot taller than me, and I hated that I had to tilt my head back to look him in the eye. "You don't get to dictate who lives here and who doesn't. All you're doing is making trouble where there isn't any."

"The *Harkers* are trouble. Period. You can't imagine what's going to come crawling back into this town with them."

"Oh, you mean the same entirely legal things you and Dad, and probably Wilder and Drake for all I know, were doing back then and not telling me about?" My voice was sickly sweet, and I was *so* tired of the past ruining the present.

"That was different," he said.

"*How*?" I wouldn't know. No one ever saw fit to fill me in.

He shook his head and glared at me with a ferocity I'd never seen from him. "Pick a side, Marybeth," he spat at me. "Get your act together and make a decision. Because I'm telling you that right now, you're dangerously close to choosing the wrong one."

And with that, he turned and stormed out of my shop, leaving me speechless.

I didn't know how long I stood there, but eventually I went through the motions of closing out the register and emptying and cleaning the crock pot that held my signature peppermint hot chocolate. I grabbed my jacket and my purse. I turned off the lights. I locked the door.

And I needed Larkin.

Are you home? I messaged her as a few people walked by me on Main Street.

Just left with Nick. What's up?

Nothing. Everything.

We're going to the diner. Want to meet us there?

There was no way I was spilling all of this with Nick listening in. I could hardly comprehend telling Gabe right now.

That's okay, I typed back. *I'll see you tomorrow.*

She sent a little worried face emoji, so I sent a heart back. And after a second, I added, *Talk to him about the marriage thing already, okay?*

Then I stood on the sidewalk for a moment. Gazing down the road, my eye caught the library.

And before I'd thought it out, I was walking through the front door.

Chapter Twenty-three

Emily

"Hey, I need to take off early." Leo poked his head around the break room door where I was willing the old coffeepot to brew faster.

"Of course, that's fine. You *are* a volunteer," I reminded him with a grin, repeating what he usually liked to say to me.

"Awesome. I want to get started on this water filtration system before I lose daylight." Leo already looked a million miles away, his head off in some cloud filled with dreams of living off the grid.

"I have no idea what that entails, but have fun." I squatted down to see the coffeepot better. Maybe if I stared at it some more, it would brew faster. I desperately needed coffee if I was going to stay awake past six tonight. I barely slept at all last night, listening to Jackson's even breathing and turning over thoughts of everything that had happened and what he'd shared with me.

It was a lot to take in.

"Oh, and you've got a guest up front," Leo added before disappearing to indulge himself in water filtration systems.

I pushed myself up to standing and left the coffee to chug along while I returned to the front of the library. A guest could have been anyone—a patron, someone finally answering that *Help Wanted* sign, my mom, Jackson. A tingle ran over my arms at the thought of him.

But I didn't expect to see Marybeth Noble scrolling through her phone while waiting for me.

"Hey," I said.

"Hey." The word was weighted. She stuck her phone into her purse. "Have you got a minute?"

"Sure," I said, trying to keep the curiosity from my voice. I gestured to the chairs behind the circulation desk.

"I feel important coming back here," she said as she settled into one.

"You know you automatically become a volunteer if you step back here," I joked.

"Do you need help? I can definitely do something while I talk. It would help me, actually."

She was serious. "Okay. Um . . ." I glanced around at the work waiting for me and gathered up a stamp and inkpad, along with a stack of brand-new paperbacks. "Just stamp the first page, then once on the top edge of the book. Like this." I showed her, and she nodded.

She was quiet as she got started. I shifted in my seat, not sure what to do and wishing for that coffee. "So . . . what's going on?" I finally asked.

"Everything. Thanks again for that text last night. I hope Gabe passed that along to you."

"He did." I hesitated a second, then asked, "Is Luke okay?"

She gave a snort and stamped down hard on one of the books. "He'll be fine."

I paused again, trying to decide if my next question was too nosy, or the whole reason she came here. "And you? Are you okay?"

Marybeth sighed and stopped stamping for a moment. "I don't know. I guess I should tell you that Luke said something about talking to the police. I don't know what that means, or if anything will come of it, but Jackson should know. Just in case."

I twisted my hands together. That wasn't good. I didn't ask him for details about the run-ins with the law he'd alluded to last night, but adding something else to that list probably wasn't the best thing that could happen. "I'll tell him."

"He came by my store just now. My brother," she clarified as she turned the stamp over in her hand.

I stayed quiet, deciding to let her continue only if she wanted.

"You know he's not a fan of me being with Gabe?" She looked up at me then, and I nodded. "Sometimes I think we're okay—and he says he *wants* us to be okay—but then he makes some snide remark or says something awful about Gabe. And it's been worse since we moved in together." She stared at the stamp in her hand as she spoke. Then she sighed and set it down as she reached for another book. "So today, he comes in, acts like he did nothing wrong last night, and basically tells me I need to *choose a side*."

I scrunched up my eyebrows. "What does that mean?"

"It's ridiculous, right?" She turned in her chair and looked at me for confirmation.

I nodded.

"Okay, good. I wanted to make sure I wasn't crazy for thinking that. And I'll tell you what he means by it. He's pretty much telling me I'm being a traitor to my family, and I need to dump Gabe, or . . ." She shrugged. "I don't even know the *or*. Like, what's he going to do? Refuse to talk to me, especially after everything I did to help him after his wife died? Not let me visit? He's already bad-mouthed me to our parents and brothers, I'm pretty sure. Is he going to write me out of his will like some kind of petty rich grandma?" She laughed a little at that.

I smiled at her. "I think you've got your answer."

She looked a little more cheerful. "Yeah. Thanks, Emily. Sorry to dump all that on you."

"It's okay," I said, and I meant it. It was nice to have someone depend on me for advice or just a listening ear.

"So . . ." The corner of her mouth curved up into a devious grin. "What's going on with you and Jackson? And—" She held up a hand before I could deny anything. "Don't tell me *nothing* because I was over there a while ago, and I know you've been staying there."

My face went hot.

"He's the guy, isn't he? The one you aren't telling your parents about?"

I looked down fast before she could see the truth written all over my face. "It's not . . . I mean, we aren't . . ."

"Uh-huh. You like him, don't you?"

I could hardly admit it was more than a crush to myself. But I'd stepped into a fight for him. I kept showing up at his house. And then last night, I hadn't pulled away when he took my hand. If I was honest, I'd say the demons that lurked in his past scared me a little, but that part of him was also dangerously intriguing. It was such a contrast to the Jackson I knew, to the way he treated me, to how I knew he saw his future here. I was basically a sliver of metal to his magnet, and as smart as I'd always considered myself, I was downright helpless where Jackson Harker was concerned.

And when I glanced up at Marybeth, I could tell she already knew. "Yes." I dragged the word out like it was painful to say.

She really smiled then, as if my confession was exactly what she needed to brighten her day. "Oh, you *are* so far gone."

I pressed my hands against my cheeks. "This is a problem, isn't it? I barely know him."

She shrugged. "Sometimes you just have to follow your heart instead of listen to your brain."

I had a feeling she was talking about herself just as much as me.

"Now let's talk about this whole no electricity thing," she started just as the front door to the library opened.

I looked up, ready to greet a patron—a patron who was my father.

"Dad!" I jumped up. He didn't come in here frequently, and in fact, I was pretty sure he hadn't stopped by since some time last year. Probably so he wouldn't have to be reminded about how his youngest child was throwing her life away as a librarian.

"Hey, butterbean." He smiled at me, and I beamed at the childhood nickname I'd never outgrow. I came around the counter to give him a hug. "Hello, Marybeth," he said when I let go. "How much can I pay you to stop selling those cookie cutters and little sprinkles? We're out of cabinet space in the kitchen."

Marybeth laughed. "Mrs. Foley keeps me in business. I'd ask you to tell her that I just got in some cute Easter-themed candies that'll go perfectly on top of brownies or cupcakes, but I'm also pretty sure I'll see her in the store later this week."

Dad groaned, but we could both tell he wasn't serious. He lived for Mom's baking.

"What are you doing here?" I asked. "Do you need a book?"

"I don't need an excuse to visit, do I?" His voice was light but his eyes crinkled at the edges. There was *definitely* something else.

And I had a really bad feeling I knew what it was.

"Well, no . . ." I said while silently bracing myself.

Marybeth seemed to pick up on the weird vibes between us and crossed to the opposite side of the circulation desk to throw away some tiny slice of paper that had fallen out of one of the paperbacks.

Dad ran a hand over his neatly trimmed salt-and-pepper beard. "I ran into Rob this morning after I finished my walk at the Reserve."

I swallowed. "Rob" was none other than Officer Robert Scott, Dad's old poker buddy.

"He said there was a commotion last night at Pine and Main, outside William Rosso's place. It was pretty much over by the time he got there, but he mentioned that Rosso said you were there. And that you left with Jackson Harker."

My heart dropped into my stomach, heavy with the lie I'd spun to my parents. Dad laughed, like what his friend had told him was impossible, but it trailed off when I didn't immediately brush it off as a case of mistaken identity or something.

I just couldn't handle the idea of lying again.

"Gabe is so grateful to Emily for doing that," Marybeth said out of nowhere.

I hadn't even heard her come back to the other side of the desk, but there she was, giving my dad her most winning smile.

"Emily happened to see what was going on when she left the library last night," Marybeth went on, Dad's attention on her now and giving me room to breathe again. "She texted me because she was worried about my brother. I came to get him and asked her if she could take Jackson home as a favor to Gabe. He's staying with us," she added quickly.

A second ticked by. Then another one. I thought I was going to be sick, waiting to see if Dad bought Marybeth's half-truth.

But he smiled at her and nodded. "Exactly what I thought. Rob was concerned, but I figured it was over nothing. Emily has a good head on her shoulders."

I was speechless over the compliment.

"I hope Luke's okay?" Dad said to Marybeth.

"He's fine," she said in a slightly strained voice, but her smile never faltered.

"Good," Dad replied.

I waited for him to ask after Jackson, but it didn't come. Was I surprised or had I just never noticed it before? Jackson was right. His family had been cast as the villains, and the Nobles were the heroes, and no one questioned it.

I'd never questioned it. But looking back, like I did when I couldn't sleep last night, I could pull out threads from the past that indicated something different from the hazy truth everyone accepted today. I'd never paid attention to it. I'd just accepted the outcome like everyone else.

Like Dad did just now.

"Dinner with Sabrina on the twenty-first, butterbean. Don't forget." Dad squeezed my shoulder before he headed toward the door.

My heart sunk for the second time in just a few minutes. Dinner with my sister, her husband, and my parents had been pending for a while now. And my mess of a life had made me forget all about it—until now. "I'll be there," I said automatically.

"Is this free?" Dad tapped a finger on the job search class flyer I had taped to the wall by the door.

I blinked at it, trying to pull my mind back toward my job. "Oh, yes. It's free. I'm teaching students and anyone else who wants to come how to search effectively for a job they want and how to navigate applications and resumes online."

Dad gave me a real, genuine smile. "That's great, Emily. Really a good thing for the community."

Then he waved and walked out the door, leaving me stunned with his second compliment in a row.

Chapter Twenty-four

Jackson

THE SKY THREATENED RAIN as I shoved my hands into the pockets of my jacket and hustled down Main Street.

It didn't matter that a few days had passed since I'd run into Luke at the Pine Street Bar, but it still felt like everyone in town was looking at me. Once upon a time, I would've met each stare, daring them to say anything. But all I wanted now was for it to go away. Luke had tried his hardest to distract me from the real reason I was here, and I wasn't going to give him the satisfaction of letting the Nobles win—again.

So I kept my head down and walked quickly toward the real estate office where I was supposed to meet Nick and Gabe. I was almost there when someone called my name.

I paused, turning to look behind me, only to see Mrs. Foley jogging to catch up. I'd known her since forever.

And she was Emily's mom.

The worst-case scenario tore through my mind, that she *knew.* She knew I was shacking up with her daughter—if it could be called shacking up when all I'd done was hold her hand and wake up with her pressed against me in the most tortuous way possible—and maybe worse, having Emily live in a place that was only a step above a tent in the woods. And now Mrs. Foley was chasing after me to give me an earful about all of it.

I stood where I was, bracing myself to take her tirade like a man and trying to figure out a way to make it seem not that bad.

"Whew, you were in a hurry!" She stopped in front of me, a little out of breath, but smiling.

She wouldn't smile if she was about to rip me to shreds. "It's good to see you, Mrs. Foley," I said cautiously.

"Here." She pulled a little cellophane bag tied with a bright pink ribbon from her bag. "Cookies."

I blinked at them, trying to figure out what was going on.

"They're for you, silly." She grabbed my hand and placed the bag of what looked like iced sugar cookies in my palm.

"Thank you?" I cleared my throat, realizing how rude that sounded even if I was completely confused. "Thank you," I corrected. "For these cookies."

She patted my hand. "You're welcome. I thought you needed some cheering up after the other night." She studied my face for a second. "You're healing up well. You must have a good nurse to look after you."

If only she knew.

Unless she *did* know and was choosing not to say anything.

My mouth opened, but I couldn't figure out what to say.

Her hand closed around my wrist and she leaned forward conspiratorially. "Don't take it too hard on Luke, okay? He's a good kid; he's just had a hard few years with losing his wife." She let go and straightened her coat. "You enjoy those cookies."

"I will. Thank you," I said again as she walked by me.

I had no idea what to make of any of it.

Thunder rumbled in the sky, shaking me out of my stupor, and I hurried on to Kyle Clemmons's real estate office.

"Aw, look, Gabe," Nick said the second the door shut behind me. "Our little brother needs cheering up."

Gabe grinned at my confusion and pointed to the bag of cookies I still carried. "You've been Mrs. Foleyed." His expression suddenly changed, and he elbowed Nick. "His girlfriend's *mom* made him cookies."

Nick laughed while I sputtered something useless like, "She's not my girlfriend."

"Bet she has no idea you've got Emily living in the dark over there with the mice," Nick said a little too gleefully.

"Shut up, would you?" I shook my head. "The whole damn town's going to find out if you keep talking about it. And I got rid of the mice."

"There's nobody in here but us." Nick stretched an arm out to indicate the empty seating area. "And Kyle, but he's back there at his computer, and he knows what we're doing anyway."

"Keep your voice down," I ground out through my teeth. "He doesn't know about Emily."

"Emily Foley?" Kyle said as he emerged from a door behind my brothers.

"No," I said quickly while Nick made obnoxious faces at me. "An ex-girlfriend. She's in real estate too."

Kyle nodded, and I could tell he didn't care. Thankfully.

He handed a document to Gabe. "I don't have a whole lot more to tell you, but that sale went through."

Nick cursed under his breath as Gabe studied the document. I peered over his shoulder to see a deed for several hundred acres to a Willow Cosmos, LLC.

"I can't tell for sure if the company is related to Chestnut Moon, but it follows their pattern," Kyle added.

"They're going to have the entire county bought up while we're over here trying to claim squatter's rights," Nick said darkly.

"Why so many properties?" I asked. "What are they going to do with all that land?"

"Clearly not ranching," Nick said, a bitter edge to his voice. I knew exactly how he felt. Seeing our ranch in the condition it was in was like someone taking a knife to my heart.

"No idea," Kyle said. "They've been tight-lipped, and they're going to the trouble of forming different companies to buy it up. If, of course, they are all related."

That was a sobering concept to think about. All this work Nick and Gabe had put into investigating the company that had bought our property, and they might have been following the wrong lead the entire time.

"They are," Gabe said, handing the document back to Kyle. "I feel it in my gut. What about Violet Barnes? Did she mention any other tracts of land?"

Kyle shook his head. "She swept in for the closing and was gone the second it was over. All I could pry out of her was that she was from Missoula."

"Local girl," Gabe said. *Local* was relative in a place as big as Montana. "I didn't expect that."

Kyle shrugged. "I'll let you know if she calls again."

Gabe thanked Kyle, and we headed back outside. Thunder still rumbled in the distance, but the ground remained dry.

"What do you think?" Nick asked Gabe.

Gabe shook his head. "I don't know. I feel like we keep hitting dead ends."

"We've got the house," I said.

"Speaking of which," Gabe said. "I found a guy who'll deal with the plumbing and the well. I'm paying him under the table, and he'll stay quiet about it."

Running water would be a step up. "Sounds good. You want to come by sometime and check the wiring with me? Make sure I don't electrocute myself."

Nick punched my shoulder. "Gotta have some light to see your girlfriend better."

"Will you drop it already?" I rubbed a hand over my bruised shoulder.

"Sorry," Nick said, eyes on my hand, and I knew he meant the punch, not the teasing about Emily. "Noble's made himself scarce lately."

"And even if he didn't, you'd leave him alone," Gabe said pointedly.

"We've got more important things to do that don't involve Luke Noble," I added. If Nick ignored us and went after him in some useless attempt at retaliation, it could throw everything off course.

Nick eyed me for a moment, almost like he was trying to gauge whether I was seriously backing up Gabe in this. Finally, he shook his head. "Yeah, I know."

"Don't mess with him," Gabe reiterated.

"I said I *know*."

A couple of seconds passed in which Nick fumed and Gabe stared him down. A drop of rain hit my face, and I pulled my jacket closed.

"I need to get back to the house," I said, breaking the silence.

That seemed to break Nick out of his funk. He gave me a stupid grin and flicked the bag in my hand. "Enjoy those cookies."

"Right. With my girlfriend. Got it." I held up a hand that might've also included an obscene gesture and then stalked off, leaving them laughing in my wake.

Chapter Twenty-five

Emily

I'D JUST LIFTED A hand to open the back door when it opened for me.

"Close your eyes," Jackson said, blocking the doorway.

"What?"

"Don't ask questions."

When I didn't, he gave me those raised eyebrows.

"All right. Just don't let me trip on anything." I closed my eyes and felt his hand wrap around mine.

"I've got you." He led me into the kitchen just a few feet and then stopped. Then he let go of my hand and gripped my shoulders from behind, turning me around to the left. "Now one step forward."

I took the step, still with no idea what he was up to.

He let go of my shoulders, then took my hand again, stretching it out. After a second, I heard a squeak and the telltale sign of running water.

"Water!" My eyes flew open just as he moved my hand under the faucet.

Jackson was grinning while I ran my hand back and forth under the clear stream in the kitchen sink. "Now we're only half roughing it," he said.

"How did you fix it?" I gazed in wonder at the sink, almost as if I'd never seen water before in my life.

"You can thank Gabe and the plumber he made a deal with. The guy came, worked his magic, and now we have water."

"This is incredible." I turned off the faucet to stop wasting the precious, wonderful water. "We can fill pots right from the sink! We can wash our hands without pouring a bottle over them. We can take *actual* showers!" The possibilities were endless.

"And in celebration, I have . . ." Jackson turned and reached into a plastic bag behind him. "For you." He held out a plush bath towel topped with bottles of shampoo and shower gel and a purple shower pouf. He pointed to the pouf and added, "I have no idea why those are better than a plain old washcloth, but I figured you'd like it."

I was smiling so much I could hardly contain myself. "I love it. Thank you!" I wrapped one arm around the shower supplies and the other one around him, and before I realized what I was doing, I kissed him on the cheek.

"You're welcome," he said, laughing, as I hugged the towel to my chest and fought the blush that tried to crawl up my face. "I even cleaned the bathroom. It'll be cold, but . . ." He gestured at the bathroom that sat on the other side of the hallway opposite the kitchen.

I took that as a cue to get out before I thought too much more about what I'd done. I shut the door behind me and examined the room in the light that streamed through the frosted window. He'd done a good job cleaning, especially for a guy. I'd been through it once, doing a basic clean as I'd done in the kitchen and the living room a couple of days ago. But Jackson had polished it up, and while it needed work, it was clean.

I shut the second door that led to the downstairs bedroom and tested the shower faucet. He was right about the cold. Without a functioning hot water heater, this was going to be a really quick shower. But I honestly didn't care. I'd let my teeth chatter and my fingers go numb just to stand under water that came from a showerhead.

I took the fastest shower on record, shivering as I stepped out of the tub. I rubbed down my hair and wrapped the towel around me—and realized I'd left all my clean clothes in the living room.

I looked down at myself. The towel covered everything, but still . . . it was a *towel*. I could just put the dirty clothes back on, I guessed. I glanced at them in a heap on the floor, and then at the bathroom door. A noise sounded from the kitchen across the hall. Jackson must have been getting something ready for dinner. If I tiptoed through the bedroom, I could grab my clothes from the living room without running into him.

Plan decided upon, I pressed the bedroom door open and slipped out, holding the towel tight around me. Another clunk sounded from the kitchen, and I moved a little faster. Opening the door to the living room, I peeked out.

Empty, just as I'd guessed.

Relieved, I crept out and walked silently over to my bag. I grabbed a shirt and—

"Good shower?"

I straightened so fast that I almost dropped my towel. Jackson stood leaning against the doorframe, a package of chicken in his hand. One corner of his mouth was lifted up in a highly entertained smirk.

"Yes." I clutched my shirt against the towel. Why couldn't he have bought wider towels? This one covered approximately two inches of my legs.

"Forgot your clothes?" That smirk inched even higher.

"Yes," I said again, because clearly I didn't know any other words in the English language.

"Some people might just put on the clothes they had on before."

I blinked at him. Was he seriously insinuating I'd come out here in a towel *on purpose*? Well, I had, I guess, but not for the reason he was implying.

He raised his eyebrows, and I knew every second I said nothing, he spent thinking he was right.

"I didn't want to put on dirty clothes," I sputtered.

"Uh-huh." He didn't believe me at all.

My face was getting hotter, and I clenched at the towel. "Will you just let me get my clothes already?"

He straightened and held up his hands, chicken and all. "Go ahead. No one's stopping you."

"Well, you have to leave first." I was *not* bending over and risking losing the towel while he stood right there.

"Why do I have to go? Unless you're wanting to change right here." That smirk had turned into a wicked grin.

I let out an irritated sigh. "I'm not . . ." I gestured at the bag and the towel.

"All right, fine. I'll go." But instead of turning around into the kitchen, he walked toward me.

I swallowed hard, my fingers digging into the towel as he approached. I should turn and run into the bedroom. But I didn't. I stood right where I was as trouble headed my way.

Jackson stopped beside me. I didn't dare look up at him.

He leaned down and whispered, "I should've bought a smaller towel."

The tension in my body ratcheted up about ten notches, but when I looked up at him, he smiled and then backed away.

"Chicken will be ready soon. Get dressed," he said. "If you want."

And then he disappeared back into the kitchen, leaving me breathless and burning in the living room.

Chapter Twenty-six

Jackson

IF EMILY WEARING HARDLY anything after a shower was torture, watching her eat dinner with a look of rapture on her face might actually have been worse.

"That was *amazing*," she said, sitting her empty Walmart plate beside her on the floor. "How did you get to be such a good cook?"

The compliment lit me up inside. I never really thought of myself as good at much of anything—anything legal, anyway. I shrugged, trying not to let her know how much her words meant to me. "I don't know. I guess I was just good at watching other people and picked it up. I'm glad you liked it."

"Well, it was amazing. Especially considering you did it on a camp stove."

I reached out for her plate and stacked it with mine before standing. "I have news on that front. Nick and Gabe are coming by tomorrow, and we're going to take a look at the wiring."

Her face brightened as she followed me into the kitchen. "But how are you going to get electricity when you don't own the place?"

"I'm leaving that up to Gabe to figure out. He's good at finding ways around things." I set the dishes in the sink and ran water over them.

Emily grabbed a sponge and squirted some dish soap on it. This had become our routine, ever since I'd bought actual plates. I cooked, she washed the dishes. So I stepped back and let her get to work.

"How come you didn't take a shower earlier?" She nodded at the other towel, still folded on the counter.

So I could see you walking around in a towel was what went through my head, but before I could say anything to make her blush, she added, "Isn't there a bathroom upstairs?"

That doused my witty comeback fast. "Yeah." I picked at a sliver of paint coming off the wall. Maybe I'd pick up some cans of paint once we got the electric up and running.

Emily must have heard exactly how much I didn't want to talk about the other bathroom, because she put down the sponge and turned around. "Is it filthy? The library closes early tomorrow. I could come back here and clean it. Maybe sweep and mop upstairs, too."

My eyes closed when she said the word *upstairs*.

"Jackson? What's wrong?" She was standing in front of me now, and when I opened my eyes, she was looking up at me in concern.

"I haven't been up there."

She glanced out to the living room, where the stairs were. "How come? Is it dangerous?"

"No, nothing like that." Although I wouldn't really know, considering I hadn't looked. "It's . . . a lot. To go up there."

It took a second, but she got it. She pushed her hands into her jeans pockets. "Is it something you need to do?"

I let out a reluctant sigh. "Yes. I mean, if I'm fixing up the house, it has to be the entire house. Not just downstairs and outside. And there's definitely something wrong with the plumbing in the upstairs bathroom, judging from the water stain on the living-room ceiling."

"Okay," she said, and I could almost see the wheels turning in her head. "Let's do it then. Get it over with. I'll go with you." She grabbed the camp lanterns from the counter and handed one to me.

"You don't have to," I said, but even as I said it I knew it was more because I'd rather put it off, not that I didn't want her going up there.

"Are you okay with me coming up there?" she asked.

I grabbed whatever courage I had left and nodded. "Yeah. Okay. Let's do it."

She smiled at me and led the way to the stairs. I followed her up, one step at a time, my hand trailing along the dusty banister.

"Been reading?" She leaned over and picked up *The Tempest*, which was right where I'd left it when I found it the first day.

"I figured that was one of yours, Shakespeare." I mustered a grin, and she rolled her eyes.

She balanced the book against one of the spindles and continued up the steps. On the landing, she paused while I joined her.

In the outline of the light cast from our lanterns, I spotted the bookcase at the end of the short hallway.

My heart almost stopped at the flood of memories.

"How is that still there?" There wasn't a stick of furniture anywhere downstairs, but here was my mother's bookcase. The one I had fuzzy memories of holding her houseplants and favorite novels. After Mom died, and Pops married Katrina, she'd kept the bookcase and Mom's books, but replaced the houseplants as they withered with various knickknacks. I always appreciated that about Katrina. She never tried to replace Mom—she just added another layer of family to this house.

My heart constricted, thinking of her and of Mom, both gone for so long now.

Emily's hand found mine and squeezed, and I drew in a deep breath. "This will surprise you, but that book probably came from this bookcase," I said.

"Does that mean you read it?" she asked.

"Maybe." I shrugged. "Or maybe I looked up the summary online." She laughed softly.

"It was my mom's," I said.

She squeezed my hand again, and then, after a moment passed, said, "Okay, where to first?"

I turned, taking in the doorways to the four rooms and the bathroom that made up the second floor. I nodded at one room where the door hung partway off its hinges. If I was ripping the Band-Aid off, I might as well start there. "That one. That was mine."

Dirt gritted under my shoes as Emily and I walked to the open door. I paused outside, taking a second to collect myself while I pretended to examine the ceiling in the hallway. It was a mess, paint peeling and water stains, but at least it didn't look ready to cave in anytime soon. The new roof should keep any more water out.

"Want me to go first?" Emily asked.

I brought my attention back to the doorway. "No, I'll go." I stepped inside, and just like that, it felt as if I'd stepped back into my childhood.

Thankfully, no furniture remained in this room. I didn't know what I'd do if I saw the old desk Ward and I had shared, or my bed pushed up under the window. All that was here was dirt, mouse droppings, and ghosts.

"Are you okay?" Emily looked up at me as I set the lantern down and tried to come to terms with the past. Everything I'd once had was gone, but I knew now that didn't have to mean my life was over.

I could still make something of it. Here. With my brothers, and this house… Maybe I could reclaim the good parts of my legacy and finally set aside the darkness and the loss.

I looked down at Emily, whose amber eyes were bright in the lantern light. Kindness radiated from her expression. She was concerned about me.

I almost dared hope she cared about me.

Because, heaven help me, I definitely cared about her.

I stopped trying to resist it and instead lifted my free hand to gently brush a strand of hair from her cheek. My fingers traced her skin ever so lightly, and she shivered.

"Cold?" I asked.

"No." Her voice trembled just a little, and I smiled, glad to know I had the same effect on her that she had on me.

"Thank you for this. Coming up here with me." I let my hand spread out across her cheek and jaw. "I'm not sure I would've done this alone."

"You're welcome," she said as I ran my thumb over her cheekbone. "It's kind of the least I could do."

I stilled my hand, not wanting her to think she needed to repay me in any way. "You don't owe me anything."

Her eyes found mine. "Okay." Then she smiled, ever so slightly. "I suppose we're even anyway, since I rescued you from that fight."

I let out a short laugh and let go of her hand to cup the other side of her face. "Woman, I already told you I don't need rescuing."

"Are you sure? Because it didn't look that way." Her hands found my chest, and a low growl sounded from somewhere deep inside me.

And in one fast motion, I dropped my face to hers.

She let out a little squeak as my lips claimed hers, and I thought I'd come undone. She was fire and I was blinded by it. I'd just barely tasted her lips when my phone buzzed with a text. It was easy to ignore when she gripped my shirt in her hands and met my mouth with the same urgency.

I could lose myself in her, entirely, I realized as she made a little noise when I teased her lips open. Lose everything and I wouldn't care, not if I had this.

Not if I had her.

She'd pressed herself against me, so close I thought I'd explode from the pressure.

Just as I moved a hand to the back of her head, a car door slammed from outside.

With a start, Emily pulled away, and I didn't care if the person outside was one of my brothers or the owner of Chestnut Moon, I'd gladly ignore them all to pull Emily back to me again.

My phone buzzed again, and I reluctantly pulled it out, knowing it was Nick or Gabe announcing their presence outside.

It was Nick. *Outside with Larkin. She wanted to bring you some brownies. We brought Diego.*

I silently held up my phone to Emily, who smiled at the message with swollen lips. She started to move toward the door. I reached out and grabbed her arm, still not wanting to put an end to that kiss.

She stood on her tiptoes, gave me a quick peck on the lips, and then said, "It could be worse. It could be my mom with more cookies for you."

Chapter Twenty-seven

Marybeth

"WANT MORE POPCORN?" I snuggled further under Gabe's arm as we sat on the couch we'd scored for free from Mrs. Garcia's basement. Gabe had to meet her son there early one morning while her husband was out with friends for their morning coffee. It was apparently a relic from his bachelor days. I still wondered how he reacted when he came home to find it gone.

"I'm good," Gabe said, pressing a kiss to the side of my head.

I dropped my head to his shoulder and returned my attention to the action movie he'd put on. Shia LaBeouf was just about to outrun the bad guys when a knock sounded at the door.

I sat up and paused the movie as Gabe stood.

"You expecting anyone?" he asked.

I shook my head. "It's probably a neighbor." We'd met the people on either side of us—an older couple and a young family—soon after we'd moved in.

Gabe made his way to the door, and I trailed after him, curious to see who it was. He paused to look out the peephole, and I just barely heard him curse under his breath.

"Who is it?" I asked, but he'd already opened the door.

A Summit County sheriff's deputy stood on our little front porch. Next to him was a Bent Creek police officer. The setting sun behind them was blinding, and I had to shade my eyes to recognize the officer.

"Evening, Creason," Officer Scott said. His gaze cut quickly to me, and he nodded. "Miss Noble."

"Good evening," Gabe said stiffly. "Can I help you with something?"

"We're looking for Jackson Harker," the sheriff's deputy said. He tapped an envelope against his other hand. "Is he home?"

I chewed my lip and waited for Gabe to respond. Jackson had used our address for his license and mail, and according to anyone who might ask, he was living here.

"He's not," Gabe said in a guarded, yet friendly voice.

"When do you expect him?" Officer Scott asked.

Gabe shrugged. "He's working construction. I don't usually ask him about his plans."

"Where's he working?" The sheriff's deputy didn't miss a beat.

"Up at the Summit Mountain Resort."

I tried to imagine them showing up there, in front of everyone Jackson worked with, and I wrapped my arms around myself.

Officer Scott looked at his watch. "Those boys are usually done before sunset. Mind if we wait outside?"

Gabe shrugged again, as if none of this bothered him at all. "Fine by me. But like I said, I don't know what he's got planned for tonight."

"Appreciate your help." The deputy nodded at us and turned to go down the stairs.

"You mind if I ask what this is about?" Gabe said.

Officer Scott paused, then he looked right at me with a smile. "Why don't you ask your girlfriend? Her brother's the one pressing charges." He turned back to Gabe. "And your brother ought to consider himself lucky. With his record, it's a shame the judge didn't see fit to issue a warrant instead."

He followed the deputy down the stairs, and Gabe shut the door after them.

"I was afraid this was going to happen," he said.

"I'm so sorry," I whispered. "I didn't think he'd really do it."

Gabe gathered me into his arms, and I sunk into him. "It's not your fault, Marybeth."

"I know, but . . . maybe I could've talked him out of it."

"Look." Gabe gently set me back and put his hands on my shoulders. "Nothing you could've said in that moment would have made him think differently. Right?"

I sighed, feeling completely helpless to do anything. "I guess so."

"What he said to you was awful. He's angry, and he's acting out, and I'd prefer you stay out of the way than get hurt. Again." Gabe's hands tightened on my shoulders.

I reached up and squeezed one of his hands as I nodded. I still wondered if there was some way I could've gotten through to Luke, but it was no use now unless I could figure out a way to convince him to retract it. But that sounded even more impossible than stopping him from pressing charges to begin with. "Should you let Jackson know?"

"Yeah." Gabe pulled out his phone. "When he doesn't show up here tonight, they'll probably find him at work tomorrow. At least he'll be ready for it."

While he texted, I grabbed my phone from the coffee table and opened it to my text messages with Luke. My fingers hovered over the phone for a moment. What could I say?

Finally, I started typing. *I know you're mad at me. Please don't take it out on anyone else.*

I looked up at Gabe peering through the blinds. "They're in for a long night," he said. "Bet you they don't stay past nine."

I tried to smile.

"Come on." Gabe nodded his head toward the couch. "Let's watch the movie."

I joined him, and I'd just started to become happily distracted when my phone buzzed.

It's got nothing to do with you. That was Luke's response. I kept waiting for something else, something more, but my phone stayed stubbornly quiet.

A few minutes later, it buzzed again. Gabe looked at me, clearly curious.

"Larkin," I said, glancing at the name that had popped up.

"Yeah, I messaged Nick too. Hopefully she can keep him in check." Gabe settled his head back on the couch, and I texted back and forth with Larkin for a bit.

The movie was almost over when another knock came at the door. Gabe jumped up, and I pushed aside the blinds to see out the window.

I could hardly believe what I saw.

"Guessing this one's for you," Gabe said, his hand on the doorknob.

"I have no idea what he's doing here. I didn't even know he was in town." I ran to the door, and Gabe stepped back.

I threw it open, and there stood my brother Drake.

"Hey, little sis." He grinned and held out his arms.

I threw myself into them. "You jerk," I said as I hugged him. "I haven't seen you in so long!"

"Missed you too," he said.

When he stepped back, I could see the deputy's car still sitting on the street out front. They must've gotten excited for a moment when Drake pulled up, thinking it was Jackson.

"I got your address from Luke. Hope it's okay I stopped by. I wanted to surprise you," Drake said.

"It's fine." I couldn't stop smiling. He looked the same as he did in his social media posts. Hair a notch darker than Luke's, green eyes, and a tiny scar at the corner of his lip, left over from a bike accident when we were kids. I gestured back to Gabe. "You remember Gabe, right?"

"Creason," Drake said in typical guy acknowledgment but with none of the warmth.

Gabe nodded a hello from where he held the door open. "You want to come in?"

"If it's all the same to you, I'll stay out here." Drake hitched his thumbs into the pockets of his jeans, not taking his eyes off Gabe.

My heart sunk. Luke had gotten to him. I knew it already, but I guess somehow I'd hoped otherwise.

"Have it your way," Gabe said. He glanced at me. "I'll be inside if you need me."

I nodded, and he shut the screen door.

Turning back to Drake, I smiled again. No matter what Luke had told him, it shouldn't be too hard to change his mind. He'd always been the one who doted on me when I was little, bringing me candy when I got grounded and slipping me extra dollars for ice cream or stuffed animals or whatever my kid-sized heart desired.

"So what are you doing here? How's Florida? Where's your shadow?" I lobbed the questions at him, unable to stop once I got started.

He laughed, the unease I'd seen on his face melting away. "Wilder's back home," he said, referring to his twin. "Probably being drowned with questions about cakes and flowers from Makayla. Florida's hot. And can't a guy just drop in to visit his family?"

"Of course. You're welcome anytime, I hope you know that. Are you staying at the ranch?"

Drake nodded, his gaze drifting to the deputy's car. "You've got company, I see."

I pressed my lips together, wishing he'd just stayed on the happier conversation I'd started. I'd rather hear about Wilder's fiancée, Drake's job, how many times a week Mom and Dad make him show up for dinner. Anything other than this mess Luke started.

Drake's eyes came back to me. "I'm worried about you, Marybeth."

"You've been talking to Luke."

"Of course I have. He's worried too. And I see why." He waved a hand at the sheriff's car.

I crossed my arms. "Did he tell you this is his doing?"

"He has a right to stand up for himself." Drake searched my face. "Are you happy?"

"Yes." I dropped my arms. "Yes, of course I am. It's Luke who can't let go of the past."

Drake's jaw worked, like there was something else he wanted to say, but he remained quiet.

"Did you come all the way here to check up on me?" I asked.

He smiled. "No, but it was part of the reason."

"Well, you can rest assured that I'm just fine. So, what's the other reason?"

Drake looked away then, back toward what I assumed was a rental car. "Just had some vacation time to use up."

He was bluffing. "Drake. You work for Dad. You can take off whenever you need to. What's going on?"

He ran a hand through his hair, and when he turned back around, he was smiling again. "Just wanted to spend some time with my family, that's all. But it's late, and your boyfriend isn't thrilled I'm out here, so I'm going to take off, okay?"

"Gabe doesn't care that you're here," I said, but Drake was already halfway to his car.

He raised a hand and said, "Have a good night, Marybeth."

He backed out of the driveway while I watched. After a minute, I heard the door shut and Gabe was behind me.

"Is he okay?"

I could've hugged him for asking that question instead of picking at the fact that Drake refused to come in. I leaned back against his chest, not really caring that the sheriff's deputy and Officer Scott were probably staring at us. "I think so."

Luke's words, burned as they were in my brain, ran through my thoughts again. *Pick a side, Marybeth.*

It was stupid. This wasn't football. It definitely wasn't a war.

But I kept my suspicions about why Drake was really here to myself. Gabe had enough on his mind right now.

Chapter Twenty-eight

Emily

BE THERE IN 5. The text came in from Jackson just as I arrived at the diner. I'd figured a night eating with the lights on was just what we needed—especially after a sheriff's deputy served him with a summons at work—and I was willing to part with a few dollars to make that happen.

Inside, I waved at Kim Snyder, who took over the diner from her mom about ten years ago, and looked for an open table. This place was like a who's who of Bent Creek at lunch and dinner, and coming in here made me remember why I stayed when so many of my friends had left. I'd rather be with people I knew, people who knew who I was, instead of a bunch of strangers.

And, I also knew for a fact that Mom made spaghetti every Wednesday, so I wouldn't run into my parents here.

"Emily!" I paused at my name.

Mrs. Collins was sitting in a booth with her husband. She reached into her purse and handed me a computer printout. "Give this to your mom and tell her it's the travel deals website I was telling her about."

"Okay," I said. "It's nice to see you. Enjoy your dinner."

I glanced at the paper before putting it in my purse. I had no idea Mom was wanting to travel. I spotted an open booth and was just about to sit when someone bumped into me from behind.

"Sorry!" a high-pitched voice said.

One that sounded *very* familiar.

I turned around, and my disappearing roommate stared back at me. Anna's eyes went a little round before she reached for her boyfriend Steven's hand.

"What, babe?" Steven's slacker voice was like nails on a chalkboard to me.

I ignored him and stared down my former roommate. "Where have you *been*?"

"Hey, Emily." She had the nerve to smile like nothing was wrong.

"Anna." I kept my voice down, not really wanting the entire restaurant to know my business. "Keith evicted us. Why didn't you tell me? And what happened to the rent? I gave you money every month!"

"Oh . . ." She clearly wasn't prepared to ever explain this to me. "I came up short. Sorry."

Sorry? That was all I got? I'd been way too nice to her. It's how I was, how I always was. I'd let Steven come in and eat the food I bought for myself, and I didn't complain. I didn't nag her to clean the kitchen when she made a mess, or to stop leaving her dirty clothes all over the living room. Even when she acted like Steven burning the carpet with a hot pan or breaking the showerhead wasn't a big deal, I'd let it go.

But honestly, I was sick of being Quiet Emily, the one who let people walk all over her.

"Sorry's not enough." I crossed my arms. "I want my money back. It should be . . ." I ran the calculation through my head. "Two thousand dollars."

Anna looked at me like I was crazy. "I don't have two thousand dollars."

"That's a lot of money," Steven chimed in.

"No one asked you," I snapped at him. A few people around us quieted and turned. An audience was the last thing I wanted, but maybe it was the one thing that would convince Anna to pay me back. I turned to her again. "I gave it to you to pay rent. If you didn't give it to Keith, then you still have it. Unless you spent it yourself." I left that accusation hanging.

"Emily, come on." Anna rolled her eyes. "I'll pay you back. Steven had an emergency. I needed it."

I glared at Steven, bane of my existence for almost two years. "Was it surgery? Because I can't think of any other reason that would warrant *stealing* my money."

"Hey, now." Steven reached out and put his clammy hand on my arm. "Anna didn't steal anything."

I went to shake him off, but he held on.

"Calm down, Emma," he said.

"Emily," I hissed through my teeth. "And *let go* of me."

"Do as she says or I'll pull you off of her myself." Jackson appeared next to me, his face hard and his glare fixed on Steven.

Steven dropped my arm, and I tried to rub away the feel of his fingers against my skin.

Jackson took a step forward, until he was staring down at Steven. "You touch her again and I'll kill you with my bare hands."

It was overkill, but it worked. Steven took a step backward, clearly cowed.

"Are you all right?" Jackson's gaze swung toward me. When I nodded, he turned back toward Anna. "This is your deadbeat roommate?" he asked me.

Anna's eyes widened, and she glanced at me. If Jackson was here, and he was willing to play knight in shining armor, I'd let him do it. Especially if it could get my money back.

"This is Anna. She owes me a couple grand," I said, the corner of my mouth rising a little.

"I'm going to pay it back," she said quickly.

"When?" Jackson asked.

"Um . . . here." Anna dug into her purse and extracted a handful of bills. She handed them to me.

"This is three hundred," I said, trying to hide the fact that I was flabbergasted she'd just given me anything.

"Where's the rest?" Jackson said. "What've you got, *Steven*?" He glowered at the man slouching beside Anna.

"Steven." Anna elbowed her boyfriend. "Give her that money."

Grumbling, he pulled some cash from his pocket.

"I get paid on Friday," Anna said. "I'll give you the rest then. I promise."

"Good," Jackson said. "Enjoy your dinner."

They scampered out the door, skipping their meal altogether, as we slid into the booth.

"Thank you," I said gratefully as I put the money in my purse. "Feel free to order the steak since I'm rich now."

Jackson laughed, throaty and deep, as he reached for my hand across the table. I let him take it, not caring who might see at that moment.

"I'm glad you showed up when you did, although I was doing a good job," I said, rather proud of the backbone I'd grown.

"You were. But on no planet was I going to stand there and let some guy grab you like that."

"I can handle guys," I said. Of course, I didn't really have *that* much experience, but Steven was more irritating and slimy than dangerous.

"I'm sure you can, but I don't stand for weasels like that touching the woman I— touching you."

I raised my eyebrows and lowered my voice. "The woman you what?" My heart thumped hard in my chest as I waited for his answer.

He smirked at me, like he wanted to brush it off with something flirty. But then his face grew serious, and he turned my hand over in his. "The woman I have feelings for."

I swallowed, letting that information sink in as I looked at our entwined hands. When I glanced back up at him, he was watching me, his dark eyes hooded and expectant.

So I gathered up my courage and told him the truth. "I have feelings for you too."

A smile split his face just then. And before I knew it, he rose and leaned over the table—and kissed me.

My brain shut down when his lips met mine. It was less urgent than the other night, when we'd been cut off so quickly, but it was no less meaningful. He was sweet and gentle, bringing one hand up to rest against my cheek while his lips searched mine. Time seemed to stop, as I clutched his hand and fell under his spell.

"You folks wanting to order, or what?"

Jackson pulled away, leaving me breathless and wanting and, most of all, *happy*.

"I'm having the steak," he said to the waitress, but his eyes were on me.

I didn't even know what I ordered, because all I could think about was kissing Jackson again.

Chapter Twenty-nine

Jackson

I'D JUST STEPPED OUT of the lawyer's office when a tiny dog darted past me.

"*Pollo*!" a woman's voice yelled.

I barely registered the fact that she'd named her dog the Spanish word for chicken before I took off after the scruffy little thing. He wasn't hard to catch up to—especially when he stopped to sniff some crunched up Fritos on the sidewalk.

I scooped him up, and the dog immediately started shaking. "It's all right, little fella." I petted the dog's head, but it didn't seem to help.

"Oh, my gosh, thank you!" The woman stopped beside me, out of breath.

"I see why you named him Chicken." I handed the trembling dog to her.

She laughed, and I realized that like half the people in this town, she looked familiar. "My grandmother named him. I got her Pollo because I read somewhere that it might help her dementia to have something to take care of." She paused a second and looked at me, the dog still shaking in her arms. "Jackson. Jackson Harker, right? It's Suzanne Dowling."

The second she said her name, I knew who she was. "How are you?"

"Good. It's nice to see you. Gabe was staying at our B&B for a while, so I saw him and Nick all the time. I didn't know you were back too."

I wondered what rock she'd been living under. News usually traveled fast in Bent Creek, and I'd been here for a while now.

Her phone dinged, and she pulled it from her pocket to glance at it. "And that's my call to come get my fussy kid." She shoved the phone back into her pocket and shifted the dog. "Come by sometime. Gran and I usually do a roast on Sundays for our guests. We've always got room for one more. Or two, if you have someone else you want to bring."

It sounded like a genuine offer, and not fishing to see if I was single. "Thanks," I said, and she waved as she walked quickly away.

I watched her leave, and then glanced at the lawyer's office. This guy was someone who'd come to Bent Creek during Nick and Gabe's senior year, when everything was falling apart. I'd barely known him, but Nick vouched for him as a good guy, and he seemed to be just that. At least, he appeared to believe me and was willing to represent me against the assault charge Luke had filed.

Despite Luke Noble, maybe Nick and Gabe were onto something about Bent Creek. Between Suzanne, Mrs. Foley, Mr. Rosso, and so many of the other people I'd run into, I was starting to see how it maybe wasn't as bad as I'd made it out to be after we left.

I walked down to Mountain Roasters, where Nick was waiting for me to fill him in. He was up at the counter, talking to Larkin, while Diego colored at one of the tables. No one else was in the coffee shop.

"Hey, buddy." I ruffled Diego's hair as I walked by. The kid had taken a liking to me the second he'd met me, and the feeling was mutual. He rewarded me with a grin and held up his coloring page for my inspection. "Excellent work," I said after I pretended to examine it closely. "I like what you did with that blue there."

Diego went back to work on the page, and I took a few more steps toward the counter, pausing when I could hear their conversation.

"It would be easier if we were married," Nick was saying. "I could add you to my policy."

"Probably not any cheaper, though," Larkin said. She looked up then and noticed me. "Hey, Jackson!"

"I can come back," I said, not sure if this was a conversation I wanted to interrupt.

"It's okay. Sonia's in the back, and I'm just about ready to leave. I have to get Diego home for supper." Larkin was taking off her apron as she spoke. "Can you pack up your crayons, Diego?" she called across the shop.

Nick watched her, his face unreadable. She came around the counter, stood on her tiptoes, and gave him a kiss. "I'll talk to you tonight." Then she ushered Diego out the door, leaving Nick and me standing in the coffee shop.

I turned to my brother. "Were you talking about health insurance?"

"Yeah," he said sheepishly.

"You're trying to get that woman to marry you because you have better insurance? You need to work on your romantic gestures."

He threw up a hand. "I don't know what else to do. I've tried everything else."

"Maybe she just needs time. You've barely been back together."

Nick ran a hand through his hair, clearly frustrated. "I know, but it wasn't like we were new or anything. I feel like we've already wasted so much time. I don't want to lose any more time with her."

"You're not. She's here, isn't she? With you?"

Nick let out an annoyed breath. "Yeah. In separate places. Did I mention she lives with her mother? Who still kind of hates me?"

I smiled, thinking of the way Nick described how tiny Jeanine Reyes got up in his face and told him in no uncertain terms that she didn't trust him. "Give Larkin time," I said again. "And stop pushing her."

"How was the meeting with Talbot?" Nick said, changing the subject, as we started walking toward the door.

"Good. He agreed to represent me. He thinks the whole thing is a crock."

"He's a good lawyer—" Nick stopped short at the door as it opened from the other side.

Drake Noble stopped in the doorway. He was surprised, that much was evident in his expression before he smoothed it over with a tight smile. "Afternoon, boys." He stepped inside and held the door open.

A flare of anger jumped inside me. It might not have been Drake who'd started that fight, but he was no better than Luke or any of the Nobles.

I took a deep breath and thought of the ranch, the house, my job at Summit Mountain that wasn't too bad, and Emily. And I doused the urge to take him down right here in the coffee shop.

Next to me, Nick tensed, and I knew he wasn't in as much control. I caught his gaze and tried to send him a message with my thoughts. *Stand down.* His eyes narrowed, and his jaw clenched, but with one last look at Drake, he stepped through the door into the sunlight.

"See you boys soon," Drake said as he let go of the door.

Nick whipped around, and I grabbed his arm.

"Not right now," I said, trying to appease him.

"*See you boys soon.* He'll see my fist in his face," Nick practically growled at the door.

"Luke's the one who deserves that," I said, partially to remind myself that Drake—despite all my suspicions—hadn't actually done anything to us. Not recently, anyway.

"He's still too much of a coward to show himself in town right now," Nick said with one last glance toward Mountain Roasters before we walked away.

"It doesn't matter," I said, reminding both of us. "We've got our own plans, right? Who cares what the Nobles are doing, so long as they stay out of it."

Nick said nothing, but I could tell he was thinking about it. But I had to make sure he wasn't going to start anything that would only end in more trouble than we needed.

"You want to get married, right? Larkin isn't going to be convinced if you're running around starting fights. Diego needs a dad. A real one," I added in reference to the kid's biological father, a real piece of work Nick had told me about.

"Fine." Nick shoved his hands into his pockets. "You're right."

"I know I am."

He glanced over at me. "As long as they stay out of our way. I can't promise anything if they don't."

"Fair enough," I said, because just barely buried under all my new hopes for the future, I felt the same way. History never really went away for good.

And I hoped I'd never need to act on it.

Chapter Thirty

Emily

"We have power!" I stood gaping at the back door.

Jackson flipped the overhead light off and then on again, and I almost squealed in delight.

"Happy?" he asked unnecessarily.

"I will *never*—ever in my entire life—take electricity for granted again." I dropped my purse on the counter and spun around, marveling at the fact that tonight I could take a hot shower and I wouldn't have to carry around a lantern just to see my way into the kitchen.

Jackson left the light on. "We'll just need to be careful not to leave any lights on upstairs, especially in the front, since we don't have anything blocking the windows up there."

"Got it." With this new development, it felt less like we were squatting and more like we actually lived here.

We. I looked away from him as my face warmed.

"Hey, do you have a few minutes?" Jackson asked.

"Sure."

"Take a ride with me?" He pulled his keys from his pocket.

"Where to?"

He made a face. "Since you helped me go upstairs, I figured you might come with me to somewhere else I've been putting off."

That got me curious. I followed him out the door, enjoying the feeling of turning off the lights before I stepped outside.

Jackson opened the passenger side of his car. "Don't judge me by this old wreck."

"Never." I smiled at him as I climbed in. My phone buzzed while I waited for him to walk around, and I pulled it out to find a text from my dad.

BB, would the library consider doing a computer skills class at the senior center?

I blinked at it as Jackson settled into the car.

"Everything okay?" he asked.

"Yeah. More than okay. I think my dad is—maybe—finally on board with my career." I stared again at the text, and then typed out an affirmative response. It was the kind of thing I loved doing, and the fact that Dad suggested it made it even better.

Jackson started the car, but instead of driving around the house to the driveway, he took us over a worn set of tracks around the old barn and away from the road.

"Isn't this how horror movies start?" I joked as I put my phone away.

"Eh. There's always suspenseful music playing, though. There's no music, so you don't have to worry." He shot me a grin as the car dipped and rose over the rough ground.

We rode slowly around what used to be pasture land, passing broken fences and bushes just beginning to bud out. After several minutes, he stopped the car by the edge of some woods. "We'll have to walk the rest of the way."

"Okay . . ." I was really curious now. I followed him into the trees. The lowering sun filtered through the mostly bare branches and the evergreens, casting a golden light over the leaf-covered ground.

We emerged into an open area that looked like it might also have once been a pasture. The mountains in the distance towered over the trees ringing the empty field, and the light cast a soothing glow over the whole scene. At the very edge of the open space, tucked away behind some trees, I could just make out a building.

"What is that place?" I pointed toward the trees.

"That's where we're going." Jackson led the way across the field, and I hurried to keep up. Just past the trees, he stopped.

I paused beside him, taking in the building. It looked like a warehouse of sorts, long out of use. "Is this a storage building?"

Jackson pressed a hand to his mouth, his eyes roving the building. "You could say that."

He crossed to the door and tried it. It opened right up. I peered over his shoulder into what looked like an empty space, but given the fact there were no windows, it was hard to tell for sure.

Jackson closed the door without going in and turned around. It looked like his mind was a million miles away.

"What is this place?" I asked after a minute or two.

"That," he said, glancing back over his shoulder at the building, "is what made the Harkers who we were."

"What do you mean?" I said the words carefully. Clearly there was something about this place that sat heavy on Jackson's shoulders.

Jackson took a few steps away, his hands in his pockets. When he started talking, he was looking out through the trees toward the pasture. "My first job—the first one Dad paid me for, anyway—was in that building. He saw I didn't have a way with the cattle like my brothers, and I was tough. I think maybe he believed if he put me to work out here, it would channel the other trouble I was getting into toward something more productive."

My breath caught in my throat as I realized what he was talking about.

"Most of the time, my job was to watch. Watch the guys who were unloading the crates, make sure they didn't help themselves. Watch the guys handling the money, make sure none of it went into anyone's pockets." He turned around then, pain written into every feature of his face.

I wanted to go to him, to hug him and tell him that was so long ago. But I could also tell that he needed to get this out, to face it head on. So I stayed where I was and let him continue.

"And the worst part was, I liked it." He closed his eyes at that for a moment before opening them. "I was sixteen and bored, and this was exciting. It meant Pops trusted me. He used to tell me to watch close because one day, when he got old and tired, I'd be taking his place. Smuggling in pills and heroin and whatever else he could get his hands on. Distributing it and making a ridiculous amount of money. It's hard for me to imagine that now, but I was *so* proud. Of him trusting me like that. Of thinking he would give it all to me when I got older."

"Of course you were," I said quietly. "We all want approval from our parents." I knew exactly how true that was, and when he looked at me, he gave me a wry smile, like he understood.

"Pops was guilty of everything that everyone in town thought he was, and more. But he was messy, hired the wrong people sometimes, and he acted on emotion. Word got around, even though none of it stuck. Carson Noble wasn't like that. He was just as deep into it, but he kept all his dirty dealings far away from his name. And he was smart. So smart he figured out a way to end everything we had and come out looking like he'd saved the town. He must've made a fortune after that and gotten out. Because as far as I can tell, the Nobles are squeaky clean now. Unless they really are just that good . . ." He shook his head, and I thought about Marybeth, finding out about all of this so recently. And about how much she really knew.

I moved forward then as his expression changed. I took his hand, and he wrapped his fingers around mine.

"It doesn't matter anyway, what they're doing or not doing, right?" I asked.

"Right," he said. "I don't want any of that. All I want is this land. Our house. The good things we had before Pops brought in the bad. And someone else to work the cattle."

I laughed at that, and he did too.

"Thank you for sharing this with me," I said as he stepped closer.

His thumb ran a circle around the back of my hand. "You're amazing, Shakespeare, do you know that? Just that I can tell you all this stuff—things that would make anyone else take a quick exit—and it doesn't freak you out."

"It takes a lot more than a murky past to scare me."

Jackson opened his mouth as if he was going to say something else, but suddenly, he stopped.

"Do you smell that?" He turned quickly around, scanning the area.

I sniffed the air. A faint whiff of smoke tinged the cool breeze. "Smoke?"

Jackson led the way back through the trees to the empty field. And there, just over the trees on the other side, against the setting sun, a thick cloud of black smoke rose in a column.

Chapter Thirty-one

Jackson

It didn't matter how fast we ran, or that I bottomed the car out on the rutted land over and over. We were too late to save the barn.

But I tried anyway. I couldn't call the fire department—not without blowing up our entire plan—so I yelled to Emily to call my brothers while I threw useless buckets of water on the fire. With any luck, anyone who noticed the smoke would assume we were burning a brush pile.

By the time Nick and Gabe and Marybeth pulled up, the barn was a total loss. We stood there, watching the last of it burn out.

"At least it wasn't the house," Gabe said.

"At least it wasn't the house," I repeated in a hollow voice.

"And no one noticed and called the fire department," he added.

Nick shook his head. "There's something strange about this. When was the last time you were in the barn?"

"Not since the first time we came by here, before I moved in." I had my hands too full with the house to worry about the barn.

"You didn't store anything out there?" Nick took a few steps toward the smoldering wood.

"No." I furrowed my brow. "You think someone set the fire?"

"That's exactly what I think. You weren't here when it started, right?"

I floundered a second, trying to figure out the best way to say I'd been dredging up the ghosts of the past with Emily out on the edge of the property. But Emily spoke up for me.

"We were out taking a walk through those trees back there," she said from where she stood behind us with Marybeth.

Nick cast a glance out across the dark fields. "That's far enough away not to hear a car pull up." He looked at Gabe, and they both started walking around what was left of the barn, toeing over smoking wood, and leaning over to inspect the ground.

"Gas," Gabe said. He pointed to the ground near where the big double doors used to be.

I moved forward with Nick, and sure enough, when I bent down, I picked up a hint of gasoline.

"You know who did this." Nick's voice was low and dangerous.

Gabe's face looked pinched, like he didn't want to comprehend the possibility. And I didn't blame him. It was a complication we didn't need.

"That means he knows I'm staying here." A dull ache throbbed in the corner of my skull. All I wanted was to be left alone. To do what I came here to do.

But Luke seemed hell-bent on not letting that happen. For all he knew, I was in the house, and that fire could've gotten out of control. I was going to have to sleep with that Glock next to the pillow. If I slept at all.

"Let's take a step back," Gabe said. "We need to find out first if it really was them. If it was, we can deal with the consequences of that when—*if*—we get there."

"How do we do that?" I asked, irritation and smoke shredding my voice.

"I can think of one way." Nick looked back at Marybeth.

"What?" she asked.

"Ask him," Nick answered.

Marybeth pulled on her ponytail and exchanged glances with Emily. "Luke and I aren't exactly on speaking terms right now."

"You don't have to ask him outright," Gabe said. "Just hint around and try to find out."

"You agree with him?" She looked at him, clearly surprised.

"Well . . . It's the only solution we have." Gabe shifted, looking uncomfortable. "There's also Drake. He doesn't like me, but he seems less angry about everything than Luke."

Marybeth pushed her lips together, looking at each of us, one by one. "Okay. Fine. But only because this could've been really dangerous. I'll talk to Drake and try to find out."

Chapter Thirty-two

Marybeth

THIS WAS A BAD idea.

I felt it all the way down to my bones, and my brother's words about choosing a side echoing in my head for the hundredth time didn't help either.

I tried to draw on the talk I'd had with Emily when Luke first mentioned that. *It doesn't matter*, I told myself. His drawing a line in the sand was dumb. He was already avoiding me—and that hurt enough, considering how close we'd been over the past two years. So what more could he do if I tried to get information from Drake about the fire?

Trying to get Drake alone without asking outright was the hardest part. I finally settled on early morning, knowing that Luke liked to get out before dawn to get some work done.

The sun was just about to rise when I pulled up in front of the garage. I gathered my purse and my courage, and made my way to the house.

I passed the open shed and went to the back door. It was unlocked, which meant Luke had gone out. I nearly sank into the doorframe with relief at that.

When I walked through the door, Drake was right there, eyeing the coffeemaker like a desperate man.

"Marybeth." He straightened and smiled at me.

There was no way he set that fire. Him or Luke. I was sure of it. I knew them both better than Nick or Gabe or anyone. Luke might be angry with me and still holding some old grudge, but he wouldn't do anything that reckless—or cruel.

But I needed to make certain.

"Hey." I nodded at the coffeepot. "I hope you made that. Because if Luke did, it'll be like drinking sludge."

He laughed and rubbed the sleep from his eyes. "I could use some sludge. Especially since Luke expects me to show up and help him."

I leaned against the counter, just happy for a moment to have him home again. "Didn't you tell him you're on vacation?"

"Luke doesn't believe in vacations." Drake reached into the cabinet by the fridge for a coffee mug. "What are you doing here this early? I didn't think you lived here anymore."

Ouch. I studied him a second, trying to figure out if he meant that as a jab. But he was entirely focused on pouring his coffee.

I stood up straight, ready to get this over with. "Did you hear something burned at the old Harker place last night?"

Drake didn't look up at me as he set the coffeepot down. "Did it?"

"Yeah." It was quiet a moment while I tried to figure out where to go from there. I hadn't really thought this through.

"Isn't that place abandoned?" he asked as he picked up his mug. He eyed me over the top of it, through the steam, and I could've sworn he was fishing for information. Whatever grudge or fear or whatever it was that Luke was clinging to, he'd fed it directly to Drake, and Drake had bought all of it.

I didn't stand a chance here.

The door opened beside me, and Luke entered.

"Marybeth." He stood there, clearly surprised to see me.

"Hey," I said weakly.

"Our sister was just telling me that the barn burned at the old Harker ranch last night." Drake said this casually as he leaned against the fridge door.

My eyes narrowed as I looked at him. "I didn't say anything about the barn."

Drake said nothing, just shrugged and took a sip of coffee. My gaze slipped to Luke, who'd pulled off his hat and set it on the counter.

My stomach felt like it was folding in on itself. There was no more beating around the bush. "Did you set that fire?" I asked Luke directly.

"I didn't do anything," he said, holding my gaze.

"Drake?" I asked, looking back at him.

He shrugged again.

I pushed my fingers against my forehead, trying to wrap my mind around what they were capable of. I couldn't. It was impossible.

"Could've been worse," Luke said as he sauntered past me toward the coffeepot.

I dropped my hand. "What do you mean?"

"Could've been the house." He calmly poured a cup of coffee. "Drake, didn't you see Jackson Harker pull up there one night?"

"Lights were blazing inside," Drake said.

I swallowed. Gabe said they'd just gotten the electricity connected yesterday. It had taken some maneuvering, given they didn't own the place. Which meant Drake had been by there yesterday . . .

What if Jackson or Emily had been in that barn? Or in the house, and the fire had spread? I felt sick at the thought of it. "Emily could've been hurt," I said in a whisper. If they didn't care about Jackson, they had to care about Emily.

Luke raised his eyebrows. This was news to him. "Maybe you want to set your friend straight, then, Marybeth. Let her know exactly what she's getting herself into. No one knows better than you, right?"

I stood there, gaping at him, while Drake watched us, saying nothing.

"Why don't you run on back to your boyfriend and tell him everything?" Luke flicked his hand at the door like he was done with me.

Finally, I found my voice. "What is *wrong* with you? I gave you *everything*. I picked you up off the ground over and over. I made sure this place didn't fall apart. I don't regret it—not a minute of it. But now that I'm finally living my life again, you've been nothing but hateful."

"Because what you're doing makes me sick," he barked. Then he took a breath and added in a hard voice, "I'm not going to owe you for the rest of my life, Marybeth."

I dropped a hand to my hip. "That's not what I'm asking for! I don't want you to *owe* me. I just want you to accept my choice. Be my brother. And for heaven's sake, leave the Harkers alone."

Luke's face was stony. I wasn't getting through to him, and that realization hurt more than anything.

"Drake?" I turned to my other brother, hoping for a voice of reason.

Drake set his mug down on the countertop. "You don't know half of what they've done, Marybeth. Or what they could do."

I blinked at him, fury creeping up inside. Yet more stuff no one ever bothered to tell me about—if it was even true. It might've all been a fabrication of Luke's mind, for all I knew.

"If it's from the past, I don't care," I said in a flat voice.

"In that case, go," Luke said, meeting my eyes with the hardest look I'd ever seen from him. "You've made your decision. Don't come back."

"Don't worry," I said, emotion lacing my voice. "You won't have to see me here again."

I slammed the door behind me, the tears burning my throat.

But I wasn't going to cry yet.

It was time I talked to Dad.

Chapter Thirty-three

Emily

I CLOSED MY EYES and groaned at how good the French toast tasted.

"Maybe I should've gotten that instead," Jackson said, his fork poised over the pile of scrambled eggs on his plate.

"You should have." The French toast was the only breakfast I'd ever gotten at the diner, and for good reason. The Snyders had a magic touch when it came to French toast.

"I'm paying this time," Jackson said as Kim Snyder dropped the check on our table. He grabbed it and tucked it under his plate before I could do anything.

I eyed him over my breakfast. "You've got an entire barn to rebuild."

He grimaced. "That'll be a while. There's still too much to do with the house."

"Still." I reached out a hand and tried to snatch the check from under his plate.

Jackson was too fast, though. Laughing, he slapped his hand on top of mine—and then refused to let go.

"I can't eat like this," I complained, but I didn't really mean it. I was never going to get tired of Jackson holding my hand.

"You have a left hand," he said with a sneaky grin.

"Emily?"

Jackson nearly choked on the eggs he'd just shoved into his mouth at the sound of my mom's voice. He yanked his hand away from mine and reached for a napkin to hide his cough.

"Mom!" I pulled my arm back and looked up at her. My heart slammed against my ribcage. She'd seen Jackson holding my hand—how could she have missed it? "What are you doing here?"

"Meeting some friends for breakfast." Her curious eyes took in Jackson, who'd finally stopped coughing. "Hello, Jackson."

"Good morning, Mrs. Foley," he said politely. "Thank you again for those cookies."

"You're welcome." She took in our plates, and her gaze came back toward me. "It looks like you two are enjoying a good breakfast."

The small talk was killing me. Apparently it was killing Jackson too, because he scooted out from the booth and stood.

"Excuse me," he said. "I'll just . . . Unless you want me to . . .?" When I nodded, he took off toward the bathrooms.

Mom slid into his place, arranging her purse on the seat next to her. "Well, this is interesting." She waited patiently for me to fill her in.

"Okay," I finally said, twisting my fingers into the napkin on my lap. "Um . . . I'm kind of seeing Jackson."

Her eyebrows rose, but there was the hint of a smile on her face. "Kind of? Or you are?"

"I am. We are." I sighed. "Are you mad at me?"

"Why would I be mad at you? I'm glad you're dating, Emily. You should be."

"Because . . ." I twisted the napkin so that it tore. "Dad basically asked me point-blank a while ago, and I said no because, well . . . we were just friends then. And because Dad looked like he wasn't really a fan of the idea."

"Because of who his father is," Mom filled in. "That boy had a tough life, and it wasn't his fault."

"He's changed," I said. It felt so good to finally tell her something that was true. "He wants more than what he thought he ever deserved, and he's working hard to make it happen."

Mom nodded. Out of the corner of my eye, I spotted Jackson emerge from the bathroom. He hovered there when he noticed Mom across from me.

"You're a smart girl, Emily. I trust you. Just let him know I'm trusting him, too."

I was so happy to hear that I jumped and wrapped her in a hug.

"Don't get too excited," she said, laughing, as I pulled away. "You're still going to have to tell your father."

My shoulders slumped. Dad was just starting to come around about my job. I didn't want to do anything that would make him go back to the way he was.

"Tonight," Mom said. "After dinner."

There was no getting out of it. Or out of this dinner with Sabrina. "Okay."

She squeezed my hand and left to join her friends at a table near the back. Jackson joined me as I sat back down.

"Do I need to keep an eye out for poisoned cookies now?" he asked, one eyebrow raised.

I grinned. I'd think about Dad later. Right now, it was enough that Mom trusted me. "Not at all. My mom likes you."

Chapter Thirty-four

Marybeth

I eyed the phone lying on the counter in my shop. I'd just opened, and it was even later in Florida.

I picked it up and found Dad's number. I was getting answers.

The phone rang once, twice, three times. I drummed my fingers against the countertop. There was no answer. I left a message, because Dad was one of those people who actually listened to voice mails. Then I distracted myself with work.

The day went on, and still nothing. Finally, just as I was closing up, my phone rang.

"Dad!"

"Hey kiddo." His warm voice, all those miles away, made me smile. It felt like a hug through the air. "How's it going? Is Drake staying busy?"

I frowned a little as I listened to his voice. "I'm good," I said slowly. "I saw Drake this morning. Luke's putting him to work on the ranch."

Dad laughed. "That's good. It'll toughen him up. He's gotten lazy."

I pressed a hand to my forehead. Dad had no idea what happened between us this morning. And from the way he rolled with my mention of Luke, he didn't know how messed up everything was between us.

He had no idea.

Luke had told Drake—and probably our other brothers—but he'd kept Dad out of it. At least where I was concerned. But about everything else, I wasn't so sure. "When's the last time you talked to Luke?" I asked nonchalantly.

"Couple days ago," Dad replied. "How come?"

Where did I start? I ran a finger over the edge of a wreath, letting the prickly plastic jar my mind into working order. "There was a fire. Over at the Harker ranch."

"Oh, yeah?"

I didn't have to see Dad's face to hear the slight tension in those words. "Dad. What's going on?"

"What do you mean?"

I wanted to scream through the phone. "With Luke and his vendetta against them. I know that's why Drake's here, even if they won't be upfront with me."

He sighed. "Kiddo, you know why he won't say anything to you."

I ground my teeth against my lip. I knew. Luke had made that abundantly clear.

"As far as everything else, I'm out of it. Completely. My business is here in Florida. You want answers, you'll have to get them from your brothers."

I smoothed out the bow on the wreath, thinking about how impossible that would be. "Can you at least tell me what you and Luke talked about?"

"Wasn't much. Just the ranch and a girl he's been seeing. Violet or Valerie or something." He paused while I tried to fathom Luke actually dating someone. He hadn't shown the remotest interest in anyone since he lost Liz. And that name . . .

"You can trust him, Marybeth. He'd do anything for you, and he'll do anything to protect his family and what belongs to us." Dad turned and whispered something away from the phone. "I've got to hang up. Your mom's got dinner ready. She says hi, by the way."

"Hi, Mom," I said mechanically.

We hung up and I stared at the wreath. Gold strands wound through shades of purple on the ribbon I'd chosen for it. Purple . . . Violet.

I couldn't wrap my mind around Luke actually seeing someone, but I was pretty sure I knew who the woman was.

Violet Barnes, employee of Willow Cosmos, a company somehow related to Chestnut Moon, who owned the Harker property.

That wasn't a coincidence. Something else was going to happen. Something bad.

I was on the phone to Gabe as soon as I locked the door.

Chapter Thirty-five

Jackson

I WAS LOOKING OUT the window into the growing darkness where the barn used to be when a pair of arms wrapped themselves around my waist.

"It can be rebuilt," Emily said in my ear.

"I know. I hate that it adds another thing to get done to the list." I sighed, ready to stop thinking about that. And when I turned around, the work ahead of me disappeared from my mind completely. "Look at you." I took her hands and held them out to better admire her.

"Is it okay?" she asked, as if she wasn't the most gorgeous woman I'd ever seen.

"More than okay." I ran my gaze down the length of her. She wore a yellow sweater that brought out the color of her eyes and a pair of tight jeans tucked into knee-high brown boots. Her hair was swept up into a neat ponytail while a pendant sparkled at her neck.

"It's just dinner with my parents and Sabrina, but I always feel so much lesser than my sister. Like, I put all this effort into what I'm wearing, but I'm sure she'll show up in something name brand and stunning, and I'll just wind up looking like . . . me."

"I like looking at you." I hitched a finger into the belt loops on either side of her jeans and drew her closer. "In fact, how about you ditch them and have dinner with me instead?"

She laughed. "It wouldn't be hard to convince me."

"Yeah?" I dropped my face to her neck, thankful for ponytails that gave me better access to that soft skin. I took a half second to breathe in the scent of her before tracing light kisses across the side of her neck.

"Jackson." She batted at me before shivering and digging her fingers into my shoulders.

"Convinced yet?" I asked before moving my lips to her jawline.

"Mmm . . ." she said as I tugged her closer.

I smiled against her skin and then gently pulled back. "I like winning, but I also like that your mother thinks I'm not terrible."

Her eyes fluttered open and she sighed. "I suppose that might change if I don't show up tonight."

"Although . . ." I gave her a wicked grin. "She has no idea you're here. For all she knows, you're too busy hanging out with Larkin."

Emily gave a throaty laugh before letting go of my shoulders. "I need to go. I'll be back soon."

"All right." I ran a hand through my hair. "I guess I'll cook something incredible and eat it all. Maybe I'll finally adopt a cat."

She brightened. "I like cats."

I had a sudden image of the two of us, curled up on a couch with a fat orange tabby between us. "A cat is better than those mice we evicted from the kitchen," I said as she slipped on a jacket.

The distant sound of tires over gravel sent the thoughts of a cat fleeing from my mind. I immediately pulled my phone from my pocket.

No texts.

"I shouldn't be later—" Emily started to say, but I held up a hand and she immediately stopped speaking. Her eyes wide, she looked at me and mouthed, *What?*

I kept my hand outstretched as my ears strained. More gravel under tires, and then, just faintly, the sound of a car door being closed very carefully.

If it was Nick or Gabe, they wouldn't be so silent. And my phone would've buzzed with a text by now.

Blood pulsing in my ears, I motioned for Emily to step back. She did, moving silently toward the door to the kitchen, while I quickly scooped up the pistol from where I'd left it by the air mattress.

I kept it at my side while I stepped softly toward the front door. If it was Luke Noble, coming back to make sure the house burned this time with us in it, I was ready.

My phone buzzed then, loud in the silence of the house. I extended the Glock out in front of me while I pulled the phone from my pocket again. If it was one of my brothers out there, they were going to get an earful.

I lifted the phone to see the text.

It was Gabe. *Get out now. Noble's got Violet Barnes in his pocket.*

My brain turned the information over fast. If Luke Noble knew I was staying here, and he told Violet Barnes . . .

I figured out who was at the door a half second before it burst open.

Chapter Thirty-six

Emily

Everything happened so fast, I couldn't keep up with it.

One second, I was pressed against the wall by the kitchen, ready to run to the back door if I had to. The next, both the front door and the back door had flown open, and what seemed like every officer on the Bent Creek police force swarmed into the house, guns drawn and yelling.

"Drop the weapon and get down on the floor!" one shouted at Jackson. Jackson immediately did as he asked, but all my brain could focus on was how that was my pediatrician's son.

"Miss! Did you hear me?" a man's voice barked at me, weirdly polite and gruff at the same time. "I said get down and put your hands behind your head."

I blinked at him. "Roger?" He'd been my chem lab partner sophomore year.

"Emily." He stared right at me, not lowering his gun. At least he knew who I was. "*Now.*"

Completely bewildered, I sank to the floor. "I'm going to miss dinner." It was the most nonsensical thing that came out of my mouth as my chem lab partner put handcuffs around my wrists.

"I'm placing you under arrest for criminal trespass and burglary," Roger said. He went on to enumerate the rights I'd heard a hundred times on TV shows, but I couldn't process any of it.

"But I'm a librarian," I said, like that was the answer to everything.

Roger said nothing to that. Instead, he wrapped a hand around my elbow to help me up.

I was being *arrested*. My stomach churned. What were Mom and Dad going to think? How was this going to affect my job? Everyone in town was going to know.

I could've drowned in the anxiety swirling around my head, but Jackson's voice broke through.

"Emily!" he shouted from where my dad's old poker buddy, Officer Scott, was pulling him into a standing position. "It's going to be okay." He held my gaze, trying to help *me* even as I knew this was going to be a lot worse for him.

I nodded, more to reassure him than myself. Because this didn't feel okay at all.

This felt like my world had imploded just as I'd started to believe it had changed for the better.

I was in a cell with one other woman, who appeared to be asleep, for only a few hours before someone came to unlock it.

"Emily Foley," the woman announced. I didn't recognize her, which was a relief in a way. I'd already seen far too many people who knew me tonight.

I stood up, ready to hear the worst.

"You're getting out," she said as the door swung open. "Bail got posted."

"Really? By who?"

She shrugged. "Heck if I know."

I didn't ask any more questions. All I wanted was to get out of here and find out about Jackson. And then take a long, hot shower to get the feel of this place off my skin. It was only as I was getting my things that I realized who must've put up the money for me to get out of here.

And sure enough, he was waiting for me.

"Dad." I wrapped my arms around myself, not sure what else to say. *Thank you* sounded awfully trite considering where I was.

"Emily." His face sagged in relief, and for the first time, I realized how much older he looked.

I didn't wait another second. I ran forward and wrapped my arms around him.

"Are you okay?" he asked.

I nodded. "I'm sorry I missed dinner."

He was quiet a moment. Then he said, "I don't understand. I feel like I don't know what's going on with you."

The way he said it tore my heart in two. And suddenly, I wanted to tell him everything. About Anna and my apartment. About Jackson. About the house. About how I'd never felt like I'd measured up to his standards. "Can we talk? Maybe outside?"

Dad gave me a sad smile. "I thought you'd never ask."

We found a bench just outside, and I started at the beginning. He was quiet as I talked, nodding here and there, frowning at points, stiffening a little when I mentioned Jackson.

"Why didn't you tell me or your mom any of this?" he asked when I finished.

I wound my fingers into the hem of my sweater. "It's just . . ." This was harder than anything else I'd already said. "I feel like I'm not ever good enough for you. Like I can't live up to your expectations. I *love* my job. I love living here. And then there's Sabrina, and . . ." I trailed off, not wanting to make it sound like I blamed her, because I didn't. "We're different people, and I wish you could see that."

"I know you are," Dad said. He shook his head. "No, I'm sorry if I ever made you feel bad for not having the same life your sister has." He laid a hand on mine, and I felt like I was six again and Dad could protect me from everything bad in the world.

It was a nice feeling. I'd missed it.

"Thank you," I whispered.

"A parent always wants the best for their child. I wanted you to have more than your mom and I do, to achieve more, be more secure, be happy."

"I *am* happy." And I was. Living in a run-down, cold house with Jackson was the happiest I'd ever been.

That might all be gone now. I swallowed the lump in my throat that rose at that thought.

"I believe you." Dad closed my hand between both of his. "I was starting to see that, especially with your work at the library. You're doing good things there, and I'm proud of you."

"Even if it'll never make me rich?"

He smiled. "*Especially* if it'll never make you rich."

"Oh, good. Because unless you've got some serious sway with the town council, I don't think I'm ever going to be a millionaire." It felt nice to joke with my dad again.

"Can I ask you a favor? Will you be patient with me?" he asked.

I was pretty sure my dad had never asked me anything like that before. "I can."

"Good." He patted my hand. "Now, about this Harker kid—"

"I was going to tell you tonight. Mom knows, and . . . Well, I promised her I'd tell you about him."

"I know," Dad said, surprising me. "Your mom told me after Rob called."

So I had Officer Scott to thank for my dad coming to bail me out. I didn't know what to think about that. "Jackson's not a bad person," I said quietly. "He let me stay at the house when I didn't have anywhere else to go. Or, I thought I didn't have anywhere else to go," I amended.

"A house he didn't own," Dad added.

"He didn't do anything wrong." I looked up into Dad's eyes, willing him to believe me. "The reason he was there was for good intentions. He wanted to fix up the house, bring the ranch back to life for himself and his brothers. And now . . ."

"You care about him," Dad said. It wasn't a question, but I nodded anyway.

"He cares about me too." I swallowed hard. What I felt for Jackson, even though we hadn't been together long, felt like a lot more than *caring*.

Dad pursed his lips together. I could tell he wasn't thrilled, but he didn't say anything.

"He doesn't deserve this," I added.

Dad was quiet a few seconds. And just as I thought he'd say it didn't matter, that Jackson was really no good, and that I'd be throwing my life away with him, he surprised me again. "I know," he said.

"You . . . You know?" Which part?

Dad gave me a soft smile. "When I got down here, I found Jackson's lawyer, and Kyle Clemmons, the real estate agent, were already here. They were talking to an officer, telling him that Jackson never broke into that house. That he'd come in through an unlocked door and was hoping to make a legitimate claim to the property by squatting."

My breath caught in my throat. Did this mean . . . "Are they letting him go?"

"Well, they have to talk to the prosecutor before any decisions can be made about charges. That goes for you, too, by the way, since you were also found to be living there." Dad slipped into a stern voice for that last bit, and I wrapped my arms around myself, trying to imagine a life in which I was an actual *criminal*, of all things.

"He's eligible for bail," Dad continued. "But since he has a court date already, and something of a history—which I hope he's shared with you, the bail isn't a small amount."

My heart deflated. I was out here, able to live my life, and Jackson was stuck inside, in a jail cell, for doing nothing wrong at all. To top it off, Dad didn't look exactly thrilled at learning about Jackson's past.

"So he'll have to stay here," I said.

"Not tonight." A male voice sounded from behind me.

I turned around—and there was Jackson.

Chapter Thirty-Seven

Jackson

Emily's arms wrapped around me while the cool night air enveloped us both was the best thing I'd ever felt.

"You're here!" She pressed her lips to mine, and just as fast, backed up and said, "How are you here?"

A throat cleared from behind her, and I quickly dropped my arms. But I took Emily's hand. I couldn't let her go after everything I'd put her through.

I looked Mr. Foley in the eye and held out my free hand. "Thank you, sir. I heard you were the one who posted bail for me."

Emily's eyes widened as she looked from me to her dad.

Mr. Foley eyed me for a moment, and then shook my hand. "I trust I didn't make a mistake."

"No, sir."

He looked at his daughter, whose hand was securely wrapped in mine. "And I trust you'll be careful with what means the most to me."

"I can promise you that," I said.

He nodded, although he didn't look entirely convinced. Then he placed a hand on Emily's shoulder. "There's a bed ready for you if you'd like it tonight."

"Thanks, Dad. I'll see you in a little while," she said in a voice thick with emotion.

He smiled at that, then nodded gravely at me and left.

The second he was gone, Emily threw herself at me again. I wrapped my arms around her, reveling in how, despite losing the one thing I came here for, I felt very lucky to have found something else even more important.

"I thought you'd be mad at me," I said, when she finally let me go.

"It wasn't your fault. I was so worried about you."

"I was fine. I was worried about *you*. You shouldn't have ever had to go through that." The image of her being led outside in handcuffs would haunt me for a long time.

"Well, I did, and I survived. But I don't ever plan on doing it again," she said with a look of distaste.

I laughed. "Not leaving the library for a life of crime. Got it."

She grinned, but then her face grew serious. "We lost the house."

"I know." I pulled her to me, pressing her against my chest. It felt like a part of my soul had been ripped away.

"What are we going to do?"

My heart warmed at the way she said *we*. Like the place meant just as much to her as it did to me and my brothers. "I don't know," I said honestly. "I'll have to talk to Gabe and Nick. We'll figure something out."

She nodded against my chest, and then straightened.

"Are you okay staying with your parents tonight?" I asked.

"Yeah." She gave a little smile. "Dad and I talked. We're good, I think. But what about you?"

"I'll crash with Gabe and Marybeth. And then I'll figure something out."

"So . . . you're staying?" she asked cautiously.

I stared at her. "Of course I am. Unless you don't want me to?" I said the last part with a half grin.

"No, I definitely want you to. I just thought that since you came here for the house, and now . . ."

I smoothed the hair that had come loose from her ponytail back from her face. "There's a lot more here for me than a house."

"Like what?" She looked up at me from beneath her eyelashes.

"Oh, I don't know. That French toast at the diner. My job. The Spring Days festival next month."

"Jackson Harker, I swear—"

"There's this cute girl who works at the library too. In fact, I think I'm falling in love with her."

Her mouth made a little "o" before she gave me the biggest smile I'd ever seen. "She might be falling in love with you too."

I touched my forehead to hers and intertwined our fingers. "Then I guess I'd better stay."

"Hmm. Only if you tell her your middle name."

I laughed. "If I do, will she kiss me?"

"She's been waiting forever."

"Douglas." I whispered it into her ear. "And don't you dare make fun of it, Shakespeare. It's a family name."

"I'd never," she said as she wrapped her arms around the back of my neck. Then she raised herself up on her toes and kissed me like she was never going to let me go again.

Which was fine by me, because I had no intention of ever being apart from her.

Chapter Thirty-eight

Marybeth

I WAS PRETTY SURE Drake was going to stand me up when he finally walked into the Snowshoe Café ten minutes late.

"I thought you weren't going to come," I said when he sat down across from me.

"I almost didn't. But then I realized that would make me an even bigger jerk than I've been, so I got in the car and came anyway." He folded his arms together on the table.

My battered heart ached at seeing him again, easing some of my anger. "I've missed you," I said. "You and Wilder and everyone else. I miss our family."

His expression softened. "I'm sorry I stayed away for so long."

I pressed my lips together and picked up my napkin, not wanting to remind him of the reason he finally came to town. Not when I had a big favor to ask of him.

"Well," I said. "You're here now."

"I am." He sat back, keeping his arms crossed, as the waitress brought us each a coffee and a plate of pastries to share.

"Thanks," I told her. I pushed the plate toward Drake. He ignored it.

"You know Luke is right to be proactive here," he said, finally addressing the wall that was between us.

I took a deep breath and let it out. "I talked to Dad. He pretty much said the same thing, but he was washing his hands of it."

"So you understand?"

I shook my head. "I don't. I don't understand why you can't just leave them alone."

"We already told you why, Marybeth. It's up to you whether you want to believe it or not."

I bit down on my lip to keep from arguing with him. They hadn't really told me anything, just hinted at vague problems from the past and made up threats in the future. But I hadn't invited Drake here to fight with him about it. I couldn't talk to Luke anymore. Drake was all I had.

"Look," I said, laying my hands flat on the table. "I know you set that fire. And I'm not here to argue with you about that or anything else. I want you to know something."

"I'm listening," he said as he picked up his coffee.

"I love Gabe. He loves me. We're together—and we're going to be together—whether you or Luke or Dad or anyone else likes it or not."

"Okay." He took a sip of the coffee. "Is that all you came here to tell me?"

"No. I also want you to know that I love you and Luke and our family. Luke might act like it's something I just threw away without a care in the world, but he's wrong. He couldn't *be* more wrong."

"I believe you. I don't like what you're doing with Creason—at all. But I believe that you still care about your family. You're my little sister, and nothing will ever change that."

My heart warmed. Maybe I had a chance here.

"I want to ask you a favor. Can you talk to Luke? Convince him to drop the assault charges against Jackson?"

Drake raised his eyebrows. "That's a lot, Marybeth."

"It isn't, though. Luke provoked him. And he wasn't really hurt. He's only doing it out of spite."

Drake watched me for a moment, then shook his head. "I can't ask him to do that."

I sank back in my chair. To say I was disappointed was an understatement. But he heard me out, and I wasn't going to push him on it. "Okay." I wrapped my hands around my coffee mug. "There is one thing I'm curious about, though."

"What's that?"

"Is Luke actually dating someone?"

Drake almost spit out the coffee he'd just taken a sip of. "What?"

"I was talking to Dad, and . . . he was under the impression Luke was dating a woman who was new to town. A Violet Barnes."

Drake's eyebrows almost disappeared into his hair. "Dad misunderstood that. Completely."

"I figured. Luke hasn't gone out with anyone since Liz . . ." I paused. What I was about to say wasn't anything Drake wouldn't already have known. "But here's the thing. I know Violet Barnes is somehow connected to whoever owns the Harker ranch. And she's the one who sent the police there that night. I figured Luke was the one who tipped her off when Dad said they were dating. Especially when that fire didn't send Jackson running."

Drake watched me a moment, almost as if he was trying to decide how much he wanted to tell me. "You're right. And I guess it doesn't hurt to say anything now, since it happened the way Luke wanted. When he started to suspect Jackson was living there, he hired a lawyer to find the owner of the place. All the lawyer could find was a connection between that company and the one Violet works for. Luke took her out to dinner once to confirm it, and then after . . ." He still wouldn't acknowledge he'd set that fire. "Later on, he let her know she had a squatter."

That made a lot more sense. Although a tiny part of my heart—the one that wasn't so incredibly angry with him—ached for Luke. Maybe if he found someone to love again, he'd quit dredging up the past to make a mess of the present. "You know, I kind of hoped Dad was right about that."

Drake gave me a sad smile. "Yeah." He took a cheese Danish from the plate. He chewed silently for a minute, and then said "I'll mention it to him, okay? About the charges. But I can't promise anything."

A smile spread across my face. "Okay. Thank you, Drake."

"Now eat one of these before they all go into my stomach." He pushed the plate of pastries across the table to me.

Chapter Thirty-nine

Emily

"It's official," Marybeth said, setting down her fork. "Jackson, you're hosting the next dinner."

"I told you everyone would like it," I whispered into his ear. It had taken some convincing for him to volunteer to bring the potato soup he'd been perfecting the last couple of weeks.

"I'm game, if no one minds sitting on the floor," he said as his hand found my thigh and squeezed. It immediately brought to mind all those dinners we'd shared on the living-room floor at the old house. The house that was now locked up tight with no one inside.

"I *ordered* the chairs already, I swear," Nick grumbled from across the table.

"From where, China?" Jackson joked.

"They're really nice," Larkin said. "You should've seen the ones he'd picked out first." She smiled up at Nick, and he smiled back. Ever since he'd agreed to move out of the Slope Motel and get an apartment with Jackson, Larkin had seemed a lot less stressed out.

The rest of the meal went by in easy conversation as we enjoyed the chicken Marybeth had made. Gabe talked about his plans to buy a smoker, Larkin shared Diego's latest adorable antics, and Jackson talked about work. I settled back in my chair, just happy to be here, with people I now considered friends.

After we finished eating, Larkin and I helped Marybeth clear the table and load the dishwasher.

"Nick seems a lot more relaxed about the marriage thing," Marybeth said as Larkin handed her a rinsed plate.

"I'm *so* glad he got a place with Jackson," Larkin said. "Sometimes I felt like he stayed at that motel because he was waiting for me."

I bit my lip, trying to decide if I should share with her some things I'd overheard. "I don't think he's giving up anytime soon," I finally said.

"Oh, I know." Larkin smiled a little, as if the thought made her happy.

Maybe she wasn't as against the idea of getting married as she had been.

"Okay, good. Because he and Jackson have been plotting something. So, just be prepared."

"But then Jackson would lose his roommate, and who would he live with then?" Marybeth looked at me as she grinned and shrugged.

"Well . . ." I handed a last dirty dish to Larkin to rinse off. "I probably wouldn't say no—"

"Of course you wouldn't," Larkin said with a smile. "You guys already shared a house together."

"I know. I guess I'm just enjoying being at home with my parents right now." Those were words I never thought I'd say, but it really had been good. Dad and I were spending more time together, and it was *nice*. And I loved having Mom around. We'd had so many good talks while I helped her with her baking. I was even helping her plan a trip to Hawaii for just herself and Dad.

But at the same time, I knew it was a temporary move. Sooner rather than later, I'd need to figure out what I was doing next—and whether I'd need to find a roommate.

Marybeth's phone dinged just as she closed the dishwasher door. "It's just Drake," she announced as she looked at her phone. "*No, definitely not tonight*," she said to herself as she typed a text back to him. She finished and set her phone on the counter. "Sorry, he wanted to come by and drop off a box of Christmas stuff he found at the house."

"How's Luke?" I asked carefully. Marybeth had been talking to Drake off and on, and things seemed mostly okay between them, but she hadn't said much about Luke lately. Only that Drake had somehow convinced him to ask the prosecutor to drop the assault charges against Jackson.

Marybeth looked at Larkin, who squeezed her shoulder in reassurance. "I don't know. He won't talk to me. Anything I know about him, I know through Drake. And Drake's headed back to Florida in a few days."

"I'm sorry. I wish there was something we could do," I said. "Some way to make him get his head back on straight."

Marybeth laughed a little. "Me too. But he told me to make a choice, and I guess he thinks I did."

"Come on." Larkin started back toward the dining room. "Let's go make sure the boys haven't completely devolved into sports talk."

As we walked back into the room, Jackson, Nick, and Gabe had congregated down at one end of the table. But they weren't talking about basketball or baseball.

They were talking about Violet Barnes.

"What's going on?" Larkin asked as she took the empty seat next to Nick.

Marybeth and I sat at the other side of the table. Jackson immediately looked at me, smiled, and took my hand. I didn't think I'd ever get tired of the feel of his hand around mine.

"Gabe's got a phone number for Violet Barnes," Nick said.

"Kyle finally weaseled one out of her. Apparently she called him again earlier today, looking for information on another property," Gabe said.

"So . . ." I looked at Gabe, then Jackson. "What are you going to do with a phone number?"

"We're not sure yet," Gabe said, sitting back in his chair as his hand rested on his phone. "I've got a few ideas, but it's going to take some more investigation."

"Of Violet?" Marybeth asked.

Gabe nodded. "I don't know how yet, but we'll figure it out."

I clasped Jackson's hand tighter before reaching up to whisper to him for the second time that night. "I also told you not to give up hope for the ranch."

"I know," he said, and he dropped a kiss to my forehead as the others continued to talk about Violet Barnes. "I love you, Shakespeare."

I smiled up at him. "I love you, too."

Epilogue

Ward Harker

I'D PUSHED IT TOO far this time.

"There's nothing else I can do." Sam Luckett, president of the company, peered at me from where he leaned back comfortably in his desk chair.

"Of course there is," I said with my usual bravado. "Look, it was just one little conversation. I've had a million just like it, and none of those were a problem."

"There are conversations that push the edge of what's legal, and then there's bribery." Sam was blunt. I had to give him credit for that. Even if I could argue nine ways from Sunday that what I'd done wasn't *exactly* illegal.

"It wasn't bribery." I waved off the idea. "It was just a . . . strongly worded suggestion."

"In your mind, maybe. But in reality . . ." Sam leaned forward. "Ward. I'm sorry about this. You're one of my best people, you know that. But I've got an entire company to run, and I can't risk it for one person."

I sat there a moment, letting reality sink in. I couldn't talk my way out of this one. And I wouldn't grovel.

"All right." I stood up and stuck out my hand.

Sam rose and shook it. "Let me know if I can put in a good word for you anywhere."

I nodded, trying to keep it together.

And I did, as I tossed everything in my office I wanted to keep into a plastic bag I had left over from a drugstore run. There wasn't much. I liked things simple.

I rode down the elevator, making stupid small talk with one of the admin assistants, and then I stepped out the door of Luckett Enterprises into the blinding Los Angeles sunshine.

All my anger converged into a pinpoint, and I started to move quickly across the street to the parking garage. Just as I opened my door to finally be alone, my phone rang.

I threw the bag into the car and yanked out my phone, glaring at the screen. It was Gabe.

I didn't have the patience for the latest family update. I tossed the phone onto the passenger seat and started the car. I was halfway through the garage when it rang again. I ignored it.

It rang again on the freeway. I ignored that one too.

It wasn't until I pulled into a spot at my apartment complex that I gave up.

"What?" I demanded into the phone when I finally answered it.

"Sounds like you're having a good day," Gabe said.

"Is someone dying? A heart attack? Bleeding out from a dog bite? Is that why you keep calling?" Gabe didn't deserve my wrath. I knew it even as I spat it out over the phone.

"Everyone's fine," he said cautiously. "You want me to call you back later?"

"No." I pressed the heel of my hand to my closed eyes as I sat in the car. "It's just been . . . a day." I couldn't bring myself to admit I'd been fired.

I was Ward Harker. I didn't *lose* jobs. Jobs came looking for me. I'd built up a name for myself, negotiating buyouts and mergers and sales.

And now I was unemployed.

A new worry rose from the ashes of my job. How was I going to tell Parker?

"Ward?" Gabe said.

I must've missed something. "I'm sorry, what?"

"I asked if you'd gotten my text."

His text. It took half a second for me to figure out which one he meant. "Yeah, the one about coming to Bent Creek?"

"Did you think about it? I figure it won't take more than a few days. You could use some PTO."

I almost laughed at that. I didn't have PTO to worry about anymore. "Sure," I found myself saying before I could even think it through. "Why not?"

"Really?" Gabe sounded surprised that I'd agreed so quickly.

I was surprised I agreed so quickly. I guess I'd have to figure out a way to tell Parker that too.

"It should be easy." Go to my old hometown and convince some chick to sell the ranch back to Gabe and my older brothers. Simple. I'd persuaded billion dollar companies to do things that weren't in their best interest, all to make a dime for Luckett Enterprises. Getting one woman to sell a piece of land in Bent Creek, Montana would be easy.

"I don't know about that . . ." Gabe trailed off. "But if anyone can do it, it's you."

I smiled at the faith my stepbrother still had in me. "Thanks. I'll start looking at flights."

"Hey, so I was talking with Jackson and Nick and . . . Have you been up to visit Pops?"

I stared out the windshield at a palm tree waving in the breeze with the Pacific Ocean mirrored behind it. Federal prison was the last place I planned to step foot in. Especially to see the man who was half the reason my life got ripped apart sophomore year of high school.

"No," I said.

"Yeah, okay. I just figured that since you're in California, maybe—"

"It's a big state," I said shortly.

"Got it," Gabe said. "I understand." And I knew he did. "See you soon."

"Hey, Ward?" Gabe said just before I could hang up.

"Yeah?"

"This one's going to take a lot of charm. And a lot of patience."

"I've got all that in spades," I said. And when we hung up, I felt strangely better.

I was *good* at my job. Sometimes too good. Sam Luckett was a coward, but I had what it took. Maybe it was time I took my talents elsewhere for a while.

Violet Barnes was going to crumble. That ranch would be ours again.

Thank you so much for reading! I hope you enjoyed Emily and Jackson's story. **Find out what happens next** when Ward makes his way to Bent Creek and finds himself in a marriage of convenience with none other than Violet Barnes, employee of the company who owns the ranch, in ***A Bent Creek Wedding***. And if you haven't read

Gabe and Marybeth's story yet, be sure to check out ***A Bent Creek Christmas***.

Come home to Bent Creek . . . a small town in Montana where everyone knows everyone, secrets live in the shadows of the mountains, and love is waiting to be found. The Harker Brothers Ranch series tells the stories of six brothers—Gabe, Nick, Jackson, Ward, Colt, and Maverick—as they return with one goal: to get the family ranch back in their hands. Reckoning with their family's past, the Nobles, and each other, each one finds love and home again in their hometown.

Join my email newsletter at catiecahill.com to keep up with everything Bent Creek.

More by Catie Cahill

About Catie

Catie lives with her family in Kentucky but half her heart is in the Rocky Mountains. Catie loves animals, planning travels, reading, and spending time with her family. Visit her online at catiecahill.com.

www.ingramcontent.com/pod-product-compliance
Lightning Source LLC
Chambersburg PA
CBHW031124130726
47988CB00006B/2221